LIVE FAST, DIE YOUNG

A NOVELLA

VANESSA BARNEVELD

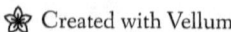 Created with Vellum

SUMMARY

Molly Corbett can't stand seeing her childhood pal Alex Gibson destroy himself. He's gone from straight-A student to rebel without a cause. With so much at stake, some serious interference is called for—or at least Micromanaging Molly thinks so. Alex needs to get back on the path to the Ivy League. But the harder Molly pushes Alex, the harder he pushes back.

Alex has a secret. Well, two secrets.

Number one: He has terminal melanoma. With six months to live, Alex hasn't got a second to waste. And hanging around hospitals when his friends think he's cutting school definitely counts as wasted time. Instead, he's going to drop out, surf, drive fast cars... and finally put secret number two out there. He's in love with Molly and he's going to tell her before it's too late.

PRAISE FOR

LIVE FAST, DIE YOUNG

2017 Aspen Gold Reader's Choice Award Finalist

Edgy, and yet wonderfully tender, LIVE FAST, DIE YOUNG sent me to reader heaven!"

I'm so impressed with how Vanessa can pack so much emotion into such a short space. A quick read, and immensely satisfying."

CONTENT WARNING

Live Fast, Die Young is, at its heart, a novella about hope and living life to the full. However, please note the story contains depictions of teens facing cancer treatment, terminal illness, divorced parents, and drug use. Readers who may be sensitive to these elements are advised to take note.

ALSO BY VANESSA BARNEVELD

Under the Milky Way

This Is Your Afterlife

Dream as if you'll live forever. Live as if you'll die today.
~ James Dean

ONE

Molly

When it comes to Alex, my best friend and study buddy, lately every little thing he does gets me steamed up. Not to mention frustrated. Confused. Sad.

All of the above.

I stop off at Burger Deluxe after school. The diner's in a pocket of coastline south of Malibu that used to be popular with tourists. Last year's wildfires scared a lot of people off for good.

My stomach rumbles because I haven't eaten lunch. Couldn't touch that cafeteria meatloaf special I mindlessly ordered. The only thing "special" about that stuff was that it resembled three-day-old roadkill.

But my main reason for coming here is not to fill up on chili fries. It's to hunt down Alex and find out why he's been avoiding me. I already checked San Marco Cove, his favorite surf spot. So this is the next logical place.

Lo and behold, the first person I see when I walk through the doors is Alex. He's facing the wall, head down.

I'd recognize the line of his shoulders and the shape of his head even in a dark room. He shaved his hair off when he was on vacation as part of some charity fundraiser. It's growing back now. Much as I miss his wavy brown locks, this crew cut looks kinda sexy.

Wait a second. I'm mad at him. We need to talk. Straightening my back, I stomp to the far corner of the dining area, bypassing the order counter.

"Alex, what are you doing here? Why weren't you in school today? You realize that's two days you've missed. In a row."

"You realize you sound like my mom right now, don't you?" But there's no real snark in his tone. Clutching his phone, he gestures for me to hop into the booth seat opposite him. His face has that weary, just-tumbled-out-of-the-surf look. He runs a hand over his cropped hair. Grains of fine white sand fall onto his shoulders.

"I'm worried, that's all. It's not like you to skip school and go to the bea—" My lips keep moving but no sound comes out, because Kip interrupts me merely by sliding into the booth beside Alex.

That's Kip as in the infamous Kip Jones. He graduated a year ago, got into community college, then dropped out after two weeks—allegedly to apply his newfound agricultural skills to growing weed. If anything, the guy is enterprising.

The guys fist-bump each other. When did Kip and Alexander 'The Geek' Gibson become pals? Alex is straight as an arrow, focused on gaining early acceptance into Yale. He wants to be a pediatrician, not a pothead.

Yet here he is, his hazel gaze vacant, spaced-out. I narrow my eyes at the remnants of burgers and chili fries on his tray. It looks like a pack of wolves tore the meal apart.

Now I'm *really* worried.

On top of steamed up, frustrated, confused, and sad. Let me add angry to that list. The two of us made plans, and now Alex seems determined to break every one of them.

Kip stares over at me and gives a slow, lazy smile. His long fingers scoop up fries. "Hey. You're Miss Molly, right? Kip."

"It's just Molly. And I know who you are," I say, my voice as frosty as Alex's untouched milkshake.

"My reputation precedes me." Kip grins, showing yellow-stained teeth.

More like your police record speaks for you, I want to say. Kip's tongue flicks out and laps sauce off the corner of his lips. Could this guy be any more reptilian? I shudder.

Turning to Alex, who's staring at his food like he's trying to figure out what planet it came from, I say, "Are you ready to go?"

He snaps out of his trance and blinks at me. "Go?"

"Yes, go." My appetite is totally out the window. Okay, I wouldn't mind swiping a fry or five. I don't do well when I skip meals. "We've got those college applications to write, remember?"

"Quit trying to micromanage me!" Alex snaps.

My jaw drops. A month ago, *he* was the one nagging me to sort out our applications. Now it's the other way around. What has gotten into him?

Kip belches and steals another handful of fries. He stares at us the same way people stare at car crashes—with morbid curiosity.

I try to ignore him. "I'm not micromanaging you. We agreed to draft our essays together weeks ago. It was *your* idea."

Alex's mouth twists. "I'm uncoupling myself from that agreement."

Rolling my eyes, I say, "Since when?"

"Since right now." He bites on a soggy fry for emphasis.

"I cannot believe you're doing this."

"It's not a big deal in the grand scheme of things," Alex insists.

"Yeah, not everyone wants to go to college," Kip adds. He sits back, hands behind his surf-tussled blond head. Grit is stuck to his elbows, making his skin look like sandpaper. "Look how I turned out. I'm livin' the dream here."

Even Alex's eyebrows rise a little at that. From where I'm sitting, Kip's living my worst nightmare. No job. No legal one, anyway. Still living with his parents. Drifting through days and doing God knows what when the sun goes down.

"I'm happy for you, really," I tell Kip, then fix my gaze on Alex. "Are you coming?"

Alex shifts his weight, but doesn't make a move to get out of the booth. His shoulders heave halfway up to his earlobes as he sighs. Suddenly, the rivers of blood-red chili on those fries are the most fascinating things in the world to him.

"Alex?"

Finally, he looks up. His gaze goes over the top of my head. "I'll see you later."

Kip chortles.

To stop my lips from quivering, I clamp them tightly together. I'm not going to blow up or cry in front of these clowns. Although... I'm close to it. In this one moment, it feels like Alex is not only rejecting our plans, he's rejecting me. And that hurts in a way I never thought possible. Like someone's rubbing salt *and* chili into a wound. Without a word, I pick up my backpack and walk out.

———

LATER THAT NIGHT, a gentle knock on my bedroom door disrupts my seventh—or is it eighth?—attempt to write a college essay.

"I'm still not hungry, Mom," I call out while staring at my blank screen. What if I write Alex's essay instead? To get the creative juices flowing? Great practice for an English lit major-to-be—

The door opens. It's not my mom at the threshold. It's the devil himself—Alex. My lungs seize.

He smiles at me sheepishly and holds up an ancient DVD case. "How about a movie? And gourmet popcorn for dinner?"

Getting over my surprise at seeing him here, I stalk to him and grab the DVD. "What's this? *Rebel Without a Cause*?"

"You've never seen it before, right? James Dean. Natalie Wood. Classic movie."

Alex snatches it back before I can read the synopsis. He crosses to my entertainment set-up—gadgets he found at garage sales and fixed up. He's useful that way. Sometimes I wonder if Alex is a genie. He won't accept a dime or even credit. I've snuck some bucks into his piggy bank when his back was turned. One day, he gave me an iPad. An iPad. And it was brand-new. Lord knows where he got it.

He gets the movie cued up to the studio's logo and takes a bag of popcorn from his backpack. Opening the bag, he waves it under my chin.

"Sweet and salty!" he singsongs. "Your favorite!"

Ugh. He knows me so well. I shove a handful of popcorn in my mouth and sit on the bed, back against the wall. "So is this your apology? Stale popcorn and a fifty-year-old movie?"

"If it's stale, why are you eating it like there's no tomorrow? And *Rebel Without a Cause* is not fifty years old. It was *made* in the fifties." He settles next to me, not close enough to touch. But I wouldn't have to lurch very far if I wanted to put my head on his shoulder. If.

"Oh, that makes it all right, then." I aim popcorn at his mouth and shoot it in. Score! This is as far as I go in terms of athletics.

"One point." He claps. "You are gonna love this. This is *the* best James Dean movie. Do you know he only made three movies?"

"Why only three?" I ask, clueless about last century's rich and famous.

Alex's voice turns flat. "He died. Car wreck. He was pretty young. Twenty-something."

"Wow, poor guy."

"Yup. He made the most of his short life, I guess." Picking up the remote, he asks, "Are you ready?"

I sigh and point to my iPad. "We should probably do those applications first."

"After the movie." He studiously brushes salt off the buttons.

"Really?" I stare at Alex. He refuses to look at me. "See, that bugs me, because I *know* how much you want to get into Yale. And to do that, you've got to apply."

"I will. Later," he says in dismissive tone. He starts the DVD player, a relic from last century that still works without a glitch.

"But college is everything to you! What's changed? Tell me!"

Finally, he faces me. "At this time, in this place, college isn't the most important thing. All we need is now."

Shaking my head, I say, "What does that even mean?"

"It means we watch this movie and forget everything else."

"But, Alex—"

"Please. Do this one little thing for me. Watch the movie. Okay? It's about kids like us. Delinquents."

"We are not delinquents. We're straight-A AP students." I cross my arms and sit ramrod straight against the wall. I'm determined to not enjoy this movie because, as far as I'm concerned, it's the one thing standing between us and the Ivy League. But as the film stretches on, I fall in love with James Dean. Long dead now. Back then? Hot. And Natalie Wood? Well, she was hot, too, in an innocent, vulnerable way. Beautiful as they were on the outside, both characters had major flaws gnawing away at their insides.

When James Dean, playing Jim Stark, gets into a huge, long, intense argument with his father, I watch Alex out of the corner of my eye. I'm sure he's thinking of his own dad, who moved back to his native Australia a while ago. Alex has stepped up his visits to "Big Dave" in Sydney lately. Each time, Alex comes back just that little bit weirder. He's starting to become a stranger. Did he and his father get into a fight during his last trip? One that the ocean-wide distance between them made even worse?

"Alex," I whisper, noticing him clenching and unclenching his fists. I inch my hand closer to his side. "Are you okay?"

His head snaps toward me. "Why are you asking me that?"

"You look sad." I pull my hand back and press the pause button. "What are you thinking about?"

He sighs and turns to me. "I'm thinking that is the worst question ever. Guys hate being asked what we're thinking."

"And gals hate resorting to reading guys' minds. It's tiring. We've got enough things to do. So to save time, why don't you just spill? Is this movie making you miss your dad?"

His hazel eyes blink. "I always miss Dad. But right now? I'm thinking I want to be like James Dean. You know, live fast, die young. Do things at full speed and go out with a spectacular crash."

"Please tell me you're joking," I splutter. Alex looks away. "Oh, God, you're serious. My friend, you are not living fast. You are sitting in one place, vegetating here slowly. And I do mean vegetating."

Squeezing his eyes shut, he puts his fingers to his temples. "Trying... to read... Molly's mind... Nope, not getting what you're saying. Spill."

"I'm talking about Kip Jones. I hear he has a particularly green thumb, if you know what I mean."

Now it's his turn to splutter. "You think I'm buying weed off Kip?"

"And smoking it? Baking with it?"

Alex laughs. "No, no, and you know I can't bake."

"Then why are you hanging out with that loser?"

"He's not a loser. He's just lost. And he looks out for me out on the waves, so..."

"Why would you need looking after? You've been surfing since you were three years old."

"Look, he just does, all right? It's the bro code." Alex turns his attention to the screen. Natalie Wood and James

Dean are looking angsty at Griffith Park Observatory. Funny—that's about an hour's drive from our neighborhood.

"Before you met Kip, you were not running around saying idiotic things like 'bro code.'"

His smile is sardonic, twisted. "This is the new me, Molly. A rebel without a cause. Better get used to it."

TWO

Alex

I leave Molly's bedroom feeling sick. Not just physically sick. The way she looked at me every time I snapped at her, it was like I'd killed a kitten with my bare hands. She doesn't deserve to be disrespected like that.

When I get to the end of Molly's driveway, I look up at her bedroom window. One second it's a blazing rectangle of yellow. Next second, it's pitch-black. I know it's dumb, but the way that light goes off, it's like she's disconnecting herself from me.

Maybe that's a good thing. Maybe that'll make things easier in the future. For her, anyway. Not seeing Molly ever again? Yeah, that's going to hurt me for an eternity.

Molly's pretty smart, but there are two things she doesn't know:

1. I'm dying. Stage IV melanoma.
2. I've been in love with her since kindergarten, since before I even knew what love is.

And there are two reasons why I don't want her to know:

1. She'll feel sorry for me and make a big fuss of things. I hate pity as much as I hate having cancer.
2. She'll say ninety percent of high school hook-ups don't last. In our case, she'd be a hundred percent dead right.

According to the docs, I *might* make it to my next birthday. So that's roughly six months to live. A hundred and eighty days. Fifteen million seconds. Still doesn't sound like much when you put it like that.

Hence all this "live fast, die young" stuff. I want to go out my way. No one, not even Molly, has the right to dictate how I should spend those fifteen million seconds.

Don't get me wrong. I don't *want* to die. Who wants to die at just seventeen?

Not me.

———————

AROUND SIX THE NEXT MORNING, I find Mom sitting at the island bench in the kitchen. She looks pretty chill for someone who just laid on a breakfast of fruit salad, yogurt, sautèed mushrooms and kale, unbuttered whole-wheat sourdough and two eggs, sunny-side up. A thick, football-field-green smoothie sits in a tall glass by the blender. Great. More kale.

"Hey, kiddo!" She smiles over her coffee mug and pats the stool next to her. "Sleep well?"

I shuffle onto the seat and stare at the food. "Have I died and gone to buffet heaven?"

My mother winces at my choice of words, then makes a big effort to put on a happy face like she always does. "I want you to keep your strength up. You don't have to eat all of it. Just most of it."

"And you don't have to go out of your way to make this for me. I mean, thanks. A lot. But I don't have much of an appetite."

"Oh, I'm having some, too," she says in an overly bright voice. With her fork, she scoops up a tiny portion of kale, hardly enough to fill a mouse's belly.

Since my diagnosis a few months ago, Mom hasn't been eating much either. This doesn't stop her from testing all the "cancer-fighting" recipes she finds on Pinterest. Baking is therapy, she says. I call it a waste of food. Fortunately, the family next door is more than happy to take excess lentil loaf off our hands.

Every hour of every day, I wonder what will happen to Mom after I go. She'll be all alone. Dad moved back to his native Australia after the divorce. He's making custom surfboards, connecting with old friends, so I know he'll be okay. Mom's literally got no one. Except the perpetually hungry neighbors and her five employees. Yet another reason why I shouldn't die so young.

It's crazy. Why does it have to be like this? Maybe the doctors got it wrong. They're not infallible. They're not gods. They can't predict the exact number of months, days, hours, and seconds a person has left on Earth.

Then again, I've peeked at my medical records. I know it doesn't look good for me. With the help of a counselor I've gotten to the stage of mostly accepting that I'm headed for a dead end. I've even started giving some of my stuff away.

The iPad Dad gave me is now Molly's. Mom won't have to go through boxes of my middle-school clothes after I'm gone because I've already dropped them off at Goodwill. The cobalt-blue board I learned to surf on? I'm giving that to a kid down the street whether he likes it or not.

Noticing I haven't touched a single morsel, Mom says, "Will you at least have the kale, broccoli and goji berry smoothie? You don't even have to chew. Close your eyes and drink it."

Speaking of acceptance... Yeah, Mom's adamant that five doctors on two continents are wrong and that I'll make a miraculous recovery. All we need is faith and love and kale.

I would rather eat broken glass mixed with cyanide, but for Mom, I guess I can manage this. Forcing a smile, I sip chunks of raw broccoli that slipped by the blender's blades. I'll check over the blender later, make sure it's working okay.

"After breakfast, I'm taking you to that appointment you missed yesterday," she says quickly.

Feeling guilty, I look away. She didn't hammer me for skipping out on seeing this "amazing herbalist-slash-psychic-healer." Still, I know she was disappointed in me. "What about work? You've missed a lot of days because of me."

"It's fine. Things are slow anyway." Her voice is two octaves higher than usual. She's lying. The real estate biz in this corner of SoCal is booming. Foreclosures have brought in the flippers—the people who swoop in on bank-owned properties and fix them up for a profit.

"But you need those commissions." Silently I add, *To pay my medical bills.*

Another reason to feel guilty. I'm aware of how much my cancer is costing my parents. Flights to a melanoma specialist in Sydney and more hospital follow-ups here don't come cheap. My folks tell me not to worry about that, but ironically I'm old enough to figure out that dying young is expensive.

And now Molly's pushing me to apply to Yale.

I can't blame her. She knows it's been my dream since forever to go to Yale, get a medical degree, become a pediatrician. But it'd be a waste of time and money for me to even try to follow that dream.

I grimace at the olive oil oozing from the barely touched kale and mushroom thing.

Waste. Sure is the theme of the day. Of my life, even.

"Alex, look at me," Mom says in a much firmer tone. "I don't want to lie to you. Money is tight, but we will manage. We always do. I have investments and savings. Your last days should not and will not be about how we're going to pay for things. So for the last time, money is not your problem. Dad and I have got this."

"Mom, I—"

She puts up a palm to stop me from going on. "Nope. Not another word about this. What I do want to hear from you is that you'll make this appointment. Today. Ten-thirty."

Glancing at the clock on the oven, I say, "So I've got time to surf."

"Or go to first period," she suggests carefully.

"You really want me to spend my final days at school? The doctors said I don't have to go."

My teachers, the principal, they all know what the deal is. Pretty soon I'll be too weak to even get out of bed let alone make it to homeroom. My parents have argued about this over and over.

Mom cups my hands in hers. I can tell by the look in her

eyes that it rips her up inside to make me choose between enjoying the time I have left and doing what normal kids should do. "You love school, remember? You can hang out with your friends. Including Molly."

"People will know something's wrong when I can't do stuff like P.E. anymore. They'll ask questions. And there's another thing. I don't want people to watch me die slowly." Or quickly. 'Cause six months isn't that long no matter what kind of spin you try to put on it.

I catch my reflection in the shiny glass of the oven door. My cheeks look less full than they did a few months ago. I've lost muscle, but apart from that I look okay. I'm over the shock of losing my hair. Everybody fell for my excuse about why I shaved it off. All in the name of charity. That was Dad's brilliant idea. Course the truth was it fell out in clumps during chemo. Shaving off the wispy leftover bits of hair was a necessity. And because I was in Australia at the time, none of my friends got to see me without eyelashes and eyebrows. I looked like an alien. Had she seen me looking like that, Molly would have figured everything out.

"Tell them the truth. The people who love you would want to help, honey. If you let them."

"No." I swig more of the craptastic smoothie. "I don't need anyone's help."

She sighs. "Does Moll-Moll know yet?"

"Mom, she's the last person I wanna tell."

"I think you're making a mistake. Please confide in her. She's your best friend." Her voice is barely audible. "You need all the support you can get."

"I'm handling it, Mom." To prove how well I'm handling it, I take a double hit of kale—first in sautèed form, then in smoothie form. The stuff tastes like bile. "You know, this kale is really giving me a ton of energy."

Mom beams at me.

"So I'm going for a surf down at the cove now."

The smile wipes from her features. "Alex..."

"Mom..." I mimic her tone, then flash her a smile. Sliding off the barstool, I say, "I've gotta do this while I can still stand up on my board."

Looking defeated, she nods.

"All right, but pick the closest surf break to the lifeguard tower. Meet me back here at no later than nine." She starts yelling because I'm already halfway upstairs. "And remember to put sunblock on."

At the stair landing, I hesitate. It's too late for sun protection now. Too late for everything.

THREE

Molly

"Unbelievable!" I glare through the windscreen with such intensity that it's entirely possible the glass will crack under the strain.

"What's unbelievable?" Suze Carlisle asks.

We're heading to school early because we have a dance committee meeting before first period. I've signed up for four extra-curricular committees this year, all in the name of college apps. As far as I know, Alex hasn't signed up for a single thing. It's so unlike him.

"Alex! He's skipping school *again*. Look!" I watch his silver Toyota streak across the intersection on the Pacific Coast Highway. His passenger? A distinctive aqua-and-black surfboard. Strapped tightly onto the roof. No prizes for guessing where Alex is heading. His words about James Dean haunt me: *live fast, die young*.

"So he's going on a surfing safari. Why do you care so much about what he does?" Suze presses the radio's volume button, muting a song I barely heard in the first place.

The subject of Alex Gibson is a touchy one for Suze. She's been my neighbor since the sixth grade and watched him come and go from my house. She used to "coincidentally" stop by for homework help while he was scrounging cookies from my mother. To call her obsessed with Alex back then would be an understatement. She badgered me to ask Alex if he liked her. That bugged me because, if you like someone, why not cut out the middleman and do the asking yourself?

Anyhow, I sounded him out, and he told me he was interested in another girl. He wouldn't say which girl, no matter how hard I needled him. At a guess, she was probably an Aussie girl he met on his regular vacations down under. I didn't tell Suze any of that. I simply told her Alex didn't have a girlfriend, which was true. Next thing I knew, she asked him out to a party.

He said no.

She didn't speak to me for a week. Like it was my fault. That was freshman year. Suze forgave me, but not Alex. Now, no matter how many other guys Suze has dated since then, every time I mention his name, she goes stiff and aloof.

"I care because we're supposed to go on this tour of colleges together, and he's completely bailed on me," I fume.

Suze's mouth falls open a little. "What? You're going away together?"

"With my mom as chaperone. It might not even happen if he keeps blowing me off. And absolutely not if his GPA goes into free fall." The Toyota is long gone. I swivel back to Suze. Her brown eyes are huge and full of curiosity.

She nods. "I knew it. I don't know how I missed it before."

"What do you know? What have you missed?"

"You've got a thing for him."

"Wh-what?"

"Come on. Don't even try to deny it."

"Suze, he's a friend. No, wait, he's like a brother because he's *extremely* annoying." The light turns green and I ease the car forward, trying to keep my attention on the road.

"Annoying, huh?"

"And he teases me too much. Like... like a brother." But do I really think of him as a brother? Not so much. I may be his best friend but that doesn't make me oblivious to his hotness. He's tall and sinewy. Got a friendly face with high cheekbones and a strong chin. A nose that isn't too broad, isn't too long, isn't bent out of shape. Then there's that mega-wide, mega-watt smile. It hasn't been as bright lately.

"Right."

"Plus, he's never talks about dating. Not when I'm around anyway."

"Okay, how does he react when *you* talk about dating?" she asks. "What happened when you went to see the new *Star Wars* movie with that sleazy guy from your chemistry class? What was his name, Declan? Deacon?"

"Deacon," I say with a shudder. Deacon who turned into an octopus at midnight. Hands. Everywhere. How I wished he'd turned into a pumpkin instead.

"Yeah, that guy."

"Alex hit the roof. I think it was because I ignored him when he said Deacon's got grabby tentacles for hands." I didn't tell Alex how badly the date went or that I almost kneed the guy. I knew he'd singsong "I told you so" when that was the last thing I wanted to hear.

Suze shakes her head and groans. "Ohhh, Molly. Don't you see? Alex has the hots for you. And you're annoyed because deep down you really like him, too, but you *tell* yourself he's like a brother."

"That's the most whacked-out thing I've heard today." So many reasons why this conversation is super uncomfortable. "He doesn't have the hots for me. I can sense when a guy likes me. Or doesn't like me, which is the usual scenario."

"That's not true, Moll."

I don't know what it is about me, but I seem to have a built-in boy repellent. Oh, they'll be friendly with me and ask for my calculus notes. I've been on a sprinkling of dates, nothing too serious. It doesn't help that Alex is *always* hanging around, I guess. Maybe people think we're a couple.

"Anyway," I continue, "even if I did have a 'thing' for Alex, which I don't, there's no way I'd act on it. That'd be the kiss of death for our friendship. Plus, lately he's been a complete oddball. One minute he's ignoring me, next minute he's barging into my room like nothing happened."

I nose the car into a prime parking space right near the door. The janitors unlock the school at seven, and it's only six forty-five now. Maybe I'm wrong about Alex skipping classes again today. San Marco Cove is only a few blocks away. There's enough time for him to catch a wave or two and then show up here before the first bell. At a stretch. Second bell, definitely.

Suze sighs. "He's cute, though. I'll give him that."

"Mm-hm." I want to say hot, but I don't. Freshman girls practically fan themselves when he grins and his dimples show. But for me it's what's on the inside that counts. I've watched him grow up into nice, dependable, smart, thoughtful Alex.

At least, he used to be.

We get out of my car and lounge on the stucco balustrades lining the entrance steps.

"Maybe he's going through a mid-teen crisis." Suze gets out an emery board and see-saws it across her black-painted nails.

"Is that a thing?"

She shrugs. "If it isn't, it should be. Some boys are off the planet. There must be a scientific, physiological explanation for it."

"Or maybe a psychological one." I gaze into the distance thoughtfully. It hurts that Alex no longer confides in me when something's *really* bothering him. After all, I was there for him when his parents split up, there when his dad moved countries, there when he and his mom had to move to a smaller house. He didn't cry and he didn't always talk about what was happening, but he never pushed me away. How did I lose his trust?

What scares me most is that we'll grow apart and lose each other. And he's already distancing himself from me.

Suze looks up and frowns. "Now that I think of it, he hasn't been as cheerful in our Asian Studies class as he usually is."

"When he bothers to come to school, you mean." Again, so not like my Alex.

Nodding, she puts away the emery board. She runs her fingers through her blonde hair, separating the carefully constructed curls. "And he's lost weight. Have you noticed?"

"He's eating plenty of popcorn, I know that," I say, picturing his lean frame. He could eat junk food three times a day and not gain an ounce. "But he's always been on the skinny side, even though he lifts weights."

"He told me he was really sick when he was little.

Maybe that's why he's naturally thin. You know, going through that might've stunted his growth."

I purse my lips. "So you know about the...?"

"Cancer?" She nods grimly. "Yeah."

Alex had a type of lymphoma when he was eight or nine. Not the terminal kind, but still... Alex missed about six months of school back then. I shake my head. "Poor guy. He spent so much time in the hospital. He hated missing school more than he hated being sick."

"That's awful. I'd hate to be cooped up like that, too."

"He didn't want anyone to feel sorry for him." I watch ants crawl over my sneaker toe. They crash into each other like bumper cars, then go on as if nothing happened. That's what Alex did when he was sick. He kept on going, kept on fighting until he beat his illness. "I remember him as the ringleader of the kids' ward, always rounding up the others for games and whatever. Sometimes they'd pretend to be in classes, because school sounded like more fun than being stuck in the hospital."

"Let me guess. He'd play the role of teacher. I bet he handed out super-tough tests," she says with a crooked smile. I sense a shift in her attitude toward Alex. Usually she tries to steer the subject away from Alex if I bring him up.

"Pop quizzes, research assignments, you name it." I chuckle, then grow serious as memories surface. "I can still picture some of those kids' faces. There was one girl named Caitlin. She was a couple of years older, but she looked like Alex's age then. Huge blue eyes in a tiny little face. Her skin was so thin you could see every vein."

"Was she terminal?"

I nod. A big lump forms in my throat. "I don't know about most of the kids in that ward, but Caitlin was definitely aware she was going to die. There was no hope left. This is what she'd tell Alex and me, 'The angels are singing to me. Listen!'"

"Oh. My. God. How freaky." Dipping her head, Suze dabs tears. "I can't imagine being that young and knowing it was all going to end."

"Yeah, her life hadn't really started." My throat constricts even more. "All she knew was the inside of a hospital. That was her world. Like, the staff did their best to turn the place into a wonderland. Bring in clowns and musicians. Make it seem colorful and fun. But when you looked closer and saw the IVs and the machines those kids were hooked up to, well, no amount of glitter was going to hide what was really going on."

Suze gulps audibly. "What happened to Caitlin?"

"Alex tried to 'cure' her," I say with air quotes.

"Um, how?"

"Well, Alex being Alex, thought he knew everything there was to know about wizardry." I smile at Suze's puzzled look. "Because he'd read all the *Harry Potter* books three times, you see. So one day, he ordered the other kids to donate their fruit drinks. All different flavors. Mixed it up with whatever food was left over from breakfast. So it was this gross, sugary, gluggy mess. He chanted spell he'd found and fed the potion to Caitlin."

Suze makes a face. "Ew. Cue projectile vomiting."

"Fortunately, that didn't happen." Poor Alex. He was only eight. And it wasn't like he'd mashed up other kids' medication into his potion. At least he had some common sense. Along with good intentions.

"Then what? Did she spit it out?"

"She loved it. Said she'd never felt better in her whole life and that it made her angels dance in a circle around her." I blow out a shuddering breath. "And then she died. The next day."

"What?!" she screeches. "Oh, please don't tell me it was because of Alex's 'magic.' It couldn't have been!"

I give her a bittersweet smile. "No, it wasn't anything Alex did. It was just an awful coincidence. No one could tell Alex that. He was inconsolable. Truth is Caitlin was even sicker than he or any of the kids knew. The doctors knew, of course. And her family."

"That is the saddest thing ever!"

"I don't think Alex got over Caitlin. If I can't forget her, chances are he can't either. He spent months with her." I wonder if she's the reason why he doesn't date anyone. Could he be holding a torch for a ghost? "Best day of *my* life was when I found out he'd gone into remission. No more hospitals. No more spells. No more gross cocktails."

"I'm sure it was the best day of his life, too." She cracks a tiny smile.

The rattle of wonky wheels and metal grabs my attention. I look over my shoulder. A homeless man in a tattered trench coat slowly pushes his shopping cart across the school driveway.

"Oh, there's Bobby Lee. Wait here for a sec, Suze." From the trunk of my car, I take a bulging laundry bag, then run to the sidewalk. "Bobby Lee? I got your clothes here, freshly laundered."

Bobby Lee walks on as if he doesn't hear me. I tap on his arm. He jumps a little, then recognition crosses his weary features. "Molly! How you been?"

"Good. And you?"

"Can't complain," says the man who's been homeless for more years than he can remember. We've been buddies since I first saw him wandering around school back when I was a freshman. He was trying to get in the main building to use the bathrooms. I snuck him in. How could I not? The man had no home, no family. There's a shelter nearby, but it's filled to capacity most days.

I hand him the laundry bag. "There's a big bottle of water in there, too. And hand sanitizer and toothpaste. And those rice crackers you like."

"Thank you, Molly. Appreciate it," he says gruffly. His face twitches as he passes me a bag of dirty clothes from the cart. He's a proud man, but he knows not to argue with me anymore about doing his laundry. I'm happy to do it. A simple thing like clean undies goes a long way to help restore a person's dignity.

"You're welcome. I'll see you next week?"

He waves and keeps walking. I stash his dirty clothes in my car. Back at the school steps, Suze is fixing her eye make-up.

I sit beside her. My thoughts turn to Alex. Like Bobby Lee, he's a proud guy. Despite the warmth of the morning sunshine, a shiver rattles my bones. What if Alex is sick again? If so, why wouldn't he tell *me* about it? What if he needs me?

No, of course, he needs me. I'm his best friend.

"It's been so hard to talk to Alex lately," I begin. "But I have to get to the bottom of what's bothering him. Maybe I should drop by and see his mom about—"

Vigorously, she shakes her head. "No, no, a thousand times no."

"Why not?" I ask, wide-eyed.

"What if she doesn't know he's been skipping school?" She slaps her forehead. "What am I saying? Of course his mom wouldn't know. Nobody skips and tells their parents. If you go behind his back, he'll hate you."

"But what if he needs my help?"

The door unlocks behind us, startling us. Inside, the janitor waves and goes back down the hall.

"Trust me. It's not worth tattling on him like some kindergartener. Talk to him face to face." Suze tugs on my arm. "Now, come on, let's get this meeting set up. I didn't get out of bed at five AM for nothing."

FOUR

Alex

I glance around the biology lab. The session with the herbalist/psychic healer was okay. I don't feel any better. Then again, I don't feel any worse.

Seems like it's been so long since I last came to class. It's really been less than a week. For extra college credit, I got a gig assisting Mr. West. It fits in well with my spare period on Fridays.

But I couldn't care less about the credit now.

In front of me, three rows of sophomore kids contemplate the dead rats pinned to boards on their benches. Joel Baker looks like he's going to throw up. Andy Redfern? Yeah, as I suspected, he's looking like he can't wait to cut out the rat's heart. Maybe unravel the intestines to measure their full length, too. He's that kind of kid.

I glance at the white rat I'd placed on West's bench. Stiff arms and legs spread out. Paws permanently curled. Pink tail in a straight line except for a tiny kink at its tapered end. Two slightly yellow teeth protrude from a vee-shaped mouth.

Gently, I prod its rib cage. Dead. I knew that. Mr. West took care of euthanizing the animals.

My stomach roils. Does this rat have a soul? Is it in heaven, looking down on its cold, dead corpse? Are we—or me, specifically—going to hell for carving up its body in the name of high school science?

Six months to live.

Six months to find out whether I'm damned for eternity.

What am I doing here?

Joel and I run out of the class at exactly the same time. He races down the hall and skids around the corner toward the bathrooms. Me, I run straight into the one person I didn't want to see.

"Alex!" Molly squeaks as she bounces off my chest.

I grab hold of her wrist so she doesn't fall backwards. "Hey, are you okay?"

She clutches her iPad tighter. "I'm surprised."

"About what? Bumping into me in school?"

"Yes, of all places!" She flashes a wry grin, then pushes long golden-brown bangs away from her eyes to peer at me. I turn my head the other way. "Maybe I should be asking *you* if you're okay. Why are you running out of class? Did the teacher spring a quiz on you and you're running 'cause you haven't studied?"

I hook my thumbs into the back pockets of my jeans. "It's D-Day. Dissection day."

Molly winces. "Oooh, not pretty. I always opt out of those. I suppose that's what you're doing now?"

"Yeah, I'm out."

She leans against a locker. "Speaking of opting out, I

really need to know, are we going on our college tour or not?"

Groaning, I try to stall her. "Don't you have a class now?"

"Free period," she says smugly. "Do you really think I'm so easily distracted that I'll forget I'm in the middle of hounding you?"

"Nope, you're persistent. Always have been." I glance down the hall again. Joel's ambling around the corner. His face is as white as beach sand. We stay silent as Joel gives us a tight, sheepish smile before going inside the lab.

"Alex, help me out here. You can't keep avoiding my questions." Molly's voice quivers. "You can't keep avoiding *me*. Something's wrong and you're not telling me what it is."

I stare down into Molly's big, big eyes. I know her so well. It's almost like I can see the confusion building up inside her. Sooner rather than later, she's going to blow her stack.

But I'm not ready to tell her. Probably never will be.

"Look, I know I've been...strange lately. But it's nothing to do with you. I'm dealing with something." I take a deep breath. "And I need to deal on my own."

She steps forward. Her hand flutters onto my arm. "Whatever it is, you can tell me. I won't judge you."

Flinching, I tell her, "Really? You won't judge me? What about the way you acted when you saw me with Kip yesterday?"

"That's way different. Kip's a real-deal delinquent. He's not the type of person you need to be hanging out with."

"There you go, judging people again."

"What if he ruins your chances of getting into Yale?" she continues.

"You don't know Kip like I do. He won't wreck my

chances." *I can do that myself.* "Don't you trust me to make my own decisions? What are you afraid of?"

Her face contorts a little, then she finally whispers, "Losing you."

Those two words knock all the air out of me. Does she *know*? Did Mom tell her?

Molly steps forward, mouth open like she's about to say something else. But suddenly, she spins on her heel and sprints down the hall.

Quickly, I try to hold onto a bank of steel lockers for support. Stupid slippery lockers. As soon as Molly's out of sight, I slide down to the floor and clutch my stomach.

This is what dying feels like. When your heart pounds hard enough to crack a rib. When loud, squealing noises echo from an unseen source. When you look around and the world distorts, fades to black. When the last thing your brain registers is the thud of your head hitting the linoleum.

I'm dead.

A FAINT BELL RINGS. Behind my eyelids, I sense a bright, flickering light. Something hard supports me. A bench. With super-thin padding. My body feels weighted down. Lifting a finger takes so much effort that I give up.

"I think he's awake."

Mom. That's my mother's voice.

Slowly, I open my eyes. Directly above me, a fluorescent light burns. Flickering. At the end of its life span.

I am not dead.

"Alex? Honey, it's Mom."

The room seems to spin as I turn toward her. The worry

lines on her forehead and around her eyes go in and out of focus. I lick my dry lips. "What happened?"

"You fainted outside your classroom." The school nurse nudges my mother aside. She takes my blood pressure. Mom and I stare silently as she checks over me.

"Who found me?" I ask in a thick voice. Please don't say Molly. Don't say Molly.

Concentrating on her work, the nurse replies flatly, "Mr. West."

"Did anyone else see me?"

"Alex, you're lucky anyone saw you at all! Stop worrying about that!" Mom says, exasperated.

"You know why I can't stop." Humiliation. Exposure. Everyone will know I'm weak. And after that, they'll treat me like a freak.

The nurse frowns at the LED display. "Another teacher saw you. They brought you to the infirmary."

When she's done looking me over, I take a few deep breaths and try to sit up.

Whoa. The room's spinning again. More deep breaths.

The nurse turns my mother. "His blood pressure is a little low, but otherwise he seems okay. His temperature's normal. I would recommend you take him to his regular physician as soon as possible, given his status."

My status. My almost-dead status, she means.

"I can still call the ambulance, if you want, Mrs. Gibson," the nurse continues. "But I don't think it's an emergency, per se."

"No, no ambulance. No doctors," I insist. "And especially no hospitals."

Mom nods. Her grip on my arm is vise-like. "I'm taking you to see Dr. Lawson now. I'll call ahead to make sure we can get an appointment."

"I'm okay. My status is fine. Let's go home." I sit up. On the inside, I scream like a drill sergeant, ordering every muscle to keep me upright. Mind over matter and all that. I glance at the nurse. "Are classes in session right now?"

"The fourth-period bell rang a few minutes ago," she says. "There shouldn't be many people in the halls."

"Great. Thanks." I feel anything but great as I walk through the deserted main corridor with Mom. She tries to put her arm around me for support. "I can move on my own."

"Of course you can." She bites her lower lip and nods. "Will you be fine to drive home, though? We can leave your car here and pick it up tomorrow."

"No, Molly will see it and wait for me, I'm sure."

"Alex, you have to stop being so stubborn about this. Molly's your friend. And she seems to be your only friend. You'll lose her if you keep alienating her."

I stare at posters lining the walls without really seeing them. Their colors and words blend into an abstract mess. "What does it matter if I lose her now or later? At least if it happens now, she won't have to see me turn into a walking corpse before I become one for real."

"Don't talk like that." She grimaces. "And despite what you think, it matters a whole lot to be surrounded by people who love you when your time comes. I know it meant a lot for both my parents when they passed on."

A pang of guilt strikes me. Like me, Mom's an only child. Grandma and Grandpa Atkins died within weeks of each other when I was twelve. They lived in a nursing home and all they had left was their daughter. Mom was really strong through the whole thing. She had to be.

Impulsively, I reach out and hug her as hard as I can.

"You're right. I'm sorry. I'll tell her. But leave it up to me, okay? I'll do it my own way, in my own time."

She nods and squeezes my hand.

We step out into the bright afternoon sunshine. Heat radiates off the concrete and cars surrounding us. Hottest February ever. Would it kill anybody to plant more trees? The spindly date palms dotted around the school aren't doing much to shade the place. But the fresh sea breeze revives me a little more.

"I'll follow you to the clinic," Mom says when we reach her car. "Give me a minute while I call Dr. Lawson's office."

I sigh. Do I really want to spend what's left of my life hanging around a doctor's waiting room?

"Can we go home? It'll be a waste of your time if we go there and can't see him," I say. "Besides, I feel all right."

She looks conflicted. "Are you sure?"

Flashing her a high-wattage smile, I say, "Yeah, I'll rest up for a while."

"You'll rest? You promise?" she asks like she doesn't believe me.

"Promise. I'll wind down, relax. Think about how I'm going to tell Molly everything."

Mom still looks skeptical, but eventually she nods. "Okay. Let's go home. I'll drive slowly so I don't lose you in the traffic."

"Pretty sure I'll find my way home if that happens, Mom."

I wave as I overtake her after the first intersection. I get to the house minutes before she does. And I didn't even have to break the 35-mile-an-hour speed limit.

"Show-off." She scowls at me when she pulls up in the double driveway. I unlock the front door and wait for Mom to go in first. "Listen, I need to check in with the office. Why don't you have a nap and I'll fix lunch in the meantime?"

Shrugging, I head to the living room and flop onto a sofa. The *Rebel Without a Cause* DVD is on the TV cabinet, right where I left it. Molly seemed to really get into the movie after a while. As for the "live fast, die young" motto? It's clear she doesn't understand where I'm coming from. How can I fix that?

Absently, I stroke the rectangular scar under my left arm. The docs cut out a chunk of tumor-riddled flesh. They said there was a chance some rogue cells migrated to my lymph nodes. They were right.

Six months to live.

Mom's right. If I have such a short amount of time left, shouldn't I spend it with people I care about? I need to fix things with Molly before she stops caring about me.

I fish my phone out of my back pocket.

ALEX

Hey.

MOLLY

Hey. Make it quick. I'm in class.

I'm not.

Why???!!!

Didn't feel like hanging around.

Say goodbye to your high school diploma!!!!!

I don't understand why you've changed since u came home from Oz.

> You can't fix me.

> If I knew what's wrong, maybe I could.

My fingers hover over the screen. I start tapping a message, then delete everything. I'd be a class-A jerk if I told her the bad news in a text.

> Have to go. Rly can't text in class. Talk later.

> K.

I scroll back up the screen and read the conversation again. It isn't always easy to know what people really mean in a text. But I know Molly. She's mad.

In the other room, Mom talks on the phone. "I'll see what I can do, Bob. But I don't... Okay, yes, yes, I get it. Okay. See you soon."

She walks into the living room and peers over the sofa. "Alex, how are you feeling?"

Wish she'd stop asking how I'm feeling. Isn't it obvious? "Fine."

Mom flicks a look at her phone. "I'm so sorry, but I have to get into the office before Bob bungles this deal. If you're hungry, there's lots of ingredients to make yourself a salad."

"Mmm, salad. Just what I feel like. Said no dying teenage boy ever." I grin to convince her it's okay to leave me alone. Mom playfully throws a cushion onto my chest.

"Please. Eat and drink something. I don't care what it is. Then rest. Love you!" She flutters away toward the foyer, purse slung over her shoulder.

"Love you, too, Mom," I say after the front door shuts. Pretty soon, I'm snoozing on the couch, dreaming about trying to break the cancer news to Molly, but being too paralyzed to speak.

A text alert rings in my ear. It's Kip.

Funny. When he was in school, we never really talked much. It wasn't until I started moping and surfing at the cove with him that I've gotten to know him a bit. He's *always* there. He doesn't pressure me. At least not about college.

KIP

Hey, man. Wanna come to the cove? Nice set of waves coming through.

My gaze falls on the DVD case again. Natalie Wood's face morphs into Molly's. She's looking at me and shaking her head in disapproval.

ALEX

Hell, yeah.

FIVE

Molly

Alex's front door swings open less than ten seconds after I press the doorbell.

"Mrs. G, I'm so sorry to bother you."

I've always called Alex's mom Mrs. G instead of Mrs. Gibson. After her divorce, I wasn't sure what to call her. But she hasn't changed her last name since the divorce, and I feel weird about calling her Jill, so Mrs. G it is.

She opens the door wider and waves me inside the house. Her hazel eyes look puffy. Red lipstick barely coats her lips, settling into fine, dry lines. She hugs me. Really, really tightly. I can feel her ribs.

"Moll-Moll, you're always welcome here. You know that."

"Thanks." My chin is jammed against her bony shoulder. Everyone seems to have a nickname for me. Only she calls me Moll-Moll. I let her cling on for a fraction longer and pull away. "Is everything okay? You're so thin right now."

Mrs. Gibson pastes on a bright smile. "Oh, everything's fine, fine! Come into the kitchen. I'm making a kale, broccoli and cucumber juice."

"Oh. Yummy." I do my best to sound super enthusiastic about the super juice. I don't have even a quarter of my mother's cooking ability, but I'm sure I could come up with a more palatable recipe.

As I follow Mrs. G to the rear of the house, I peek left and right into the dining and living rooms. Alex and his mom recently moved, so now they're only three blocks from my house instead of four. The rooms are smaller than those in the old hacienda-style place. Their furniture looks huge and clumsy in this ranch house. Not once has Alex complained about the downsides of downsizing.

"Is Alex here?"

"He'll be back. Soon. I think," she replies, striding around the timber kitchen island. There's that bright smile again. Quickly, she turns on the blender. We watch green blobs whiz around in the glass chamber until they liquefy. "Do you like coconut water?"

Shrugging, I say, "I've never tried it before."

I've never seen her act like this before, either.

"Never?" Mrs. Gibson gasps. She gradually adds the slightly opaque coconut water to the mix. "It's wonderful. So incredibly nutritious."

"Are you on a health kick, Mrs. G?"

"I'm trying to stay healthy. Do you know that one cup of raw kale contains eighty milligrams of vitamin C? That's almost as much as a whole orange!"

"Wow!" I'd much rather eat an orange, but I don't tell her that. "I can't wait to try it. I'll get the glasses."

"Thanks, sweetie. You know where to find them."

I pace around the island and grab a pair of tall glasses

from an upper cabinet. On the counter beside the fridge, amber prescription bottles stand lined up like bowling pins. It's an awful lot of pills. A cat calendar stuck on the side of the stainless steel fridge. Days are marked off with thick red marker pen. Appointments with Dr. This and Dr. That.

A cold, shivery feeling overwhelms me. Only sick people need that much medication. Are they Alex's? Or his mom's? I steal another glance at Mrs. G. Her pencil skirt is practically falling off her. She keeps hitching it up at the waist. And her cheeks look hollow, like she hasn't consumed anything but smoothies in months.

If she *is* sick, that could explain why Alex has missed so much school lately. He's probably staying home to look after her. And surfing is the only thing that takes his mind off his problems, so he spends whatever precious time he's got left at the beach. That *has* to be it.

Before I get a chance to peek at the labels on the pill bottles, Mrs. G swoops over and takes hold of my arm.

"Moll-Moll, it is *such* a lovely warm day. Let's drink these outside." She leads the way through a set of sliding doors onto the patio.

We recline side by side on redwood garden chairs under the shade of a pergola. Long tendrils of a wisteria vine curl down through the rafters, tickling my head. But all I can think about is the pill stash. My heart twinges. Alex shouldn't have to deal with his mom's illness alone.

"Cheers!" says Mrs. G, reaching out to clink her glass against mine.

I lift my glass, and the tip of a vine dunks into the drink. Gingerly, I remove the vine and take the tiniest of sips.

"What do you think?" Mrs. G asks. Her glass is now half-empty. "Refreshing, huh? Alex can't get enough of this stuff. He practically begs me to make it for him every morning."

"He should be making it for *you!*" I blurt. Mrs. G doesn't respond. In fact, silence sets in fast. There's only the sound of birds tweeting, a mower whirring in the distance, and us breathing.

All of a sudden I feel really awkward. It's not that I'm uncomfortable around her. She's like a second mom to me. But right now it's like she's wound up tight like piano wire and trying so hard not to snap. At the same time, she's pretending nothing's wrong.

Question is, do I ask her what's on her mind? What would be the harm? Maybe I could help. Unless relationship problems are the cause of her scary weight loss. I'm not the best person to talk to about romance. If she goes into too-much-information territory, then the awkwardness level would be off the scale.

No, I should just be quiet until Alex comes home. Concentrate on something else. I put my glass on the chair's armrest and set about twisting some of the wisteria vines out of the way. Once that's done, I pluck three varieties of weeds from the gaps between flagstones.

"You don't have to do that!" she exclaims. Talk about a delayed reaction. Something's *really* up with her.

"It's totally fine, Mrs. G," I reply in a super-cheerful voice. "Weeding is therapeutic."

"Absolutely. I should do it more often," she says after a long pause. Mrs. G stares at my hands, but in an unfocused way. As if she's thinking about something completely different. Her face is pale. Way too pale for Southern California. The make-up she's wearing is doing nothing to conceal the purple smudges beneath her eyes. Spindly fingers continuously spin a ring on her right hand. It's her wedding band, I realize.

Tossing the weeds on a patch of hot concrete, I sit back on my heels. "Mrs. G?"

She clears her throat. "Yes, Moll-Moll?"

"I don't mean to pry, but..." She looks away. Probably because she's aware I'm going to do just that. Pry. She knows I like to make everything my business. Some people think I'm nosy. I say it's because I care enough to help people deal with their problems. My pulse gallops. I've started this conversation and now I can't stop it. "Are you unwell?"

She stares at me eyes wide. Her fingers work that ring even faster now. "Me? Sick?"

"I, um, saw all those pill bottles on the kitchen counter and I wondered..." I drop my gaze and rip out a few more weeds around my chair's legs.

Mrs. G looks uncertain for a split-second. "They're, uh, hormone pills. You know? For menopause."

"Oh." I blink. Mrs. G is forty-something, around the same age as Mom. Granny Corbett, my paternal grandmother, was almost sixty when she went through "the change." Believe me, everybody knew about it. The mailman. The packers at the grocery store. My ballet teacher. Everybody.

Mrs. G picks up her glass and knocks the rest of her monster-green drink back in one hit. Her hand trembles. Enough for me to notice without looking too closely. "The kale smoothies really help bring some relief to those hot flashes."

So Alex is okay, then. That's a relief. His cancer isn't back. Of course it isn't. He beat that thing into submission years ago. But... *all* those pills are for menopause? Really?

Sheepishly, I say, "Sorry for pushing you into telling me something so personal."

"Don't be sorry," Mrs. G says, patting my now dirty hand. She stands and collects our glasses. "Will you excuse me? I need to make a phone call. Stay right here, and I'll be back soon with another smoothie, okay?"

I smile. "Sure. Thanks, Mrs. G."

"Stay right here." Her smile is bright and white and overly perky.

Mrs. G can't get inside fast enough, almost tripping over the threshold. I bet she's as embarrassed as I am. She shuts the French doors. Some clunking and rattling echoes through the kitchen, then I hear the sound of high-heeled shoes hurrying across hardwood.

Five, ten minutes pass. There's not a lot of shade under the pergola now. I could really do with a drink. Something crystal clear and old-fashioned. Like water. I wander into the kitchen. After scrubbing dirt and weeds off my hands, I help myself to the fridge's ice and water dispenser. That's when I notice not only is the cat calendar gone, so is the cache of pills. Totally obvious that Mrs. G thought there was a high chance I'd try to get a closer look at those things.

She was right, of course.

Her soft voice floats down from her bedroom. It's hard to make out her conversation, but I hear Alex's name at least three times. Discreetly, I head back to the patio. Minutes later, Mrs. G returns. And without the promised kale concoction.

She sits prim as a princess, then leans back, then fidgets wildly and stands up. Her face is a picture of worry, all lines and creases.

"Tough phone call, Mrs. G?"

My question seems to startle her. She practically jumps

out of her skin. She settles down enough to nod a couple of times. Looking down at her lap, she says, "You ever get frustrated with someone? Someone you really love and adore? And you know you have a right to be angry with them, but at the same time, you don't want to upset the balance because life's... too short?"

"Oh, yeah," I say, thinking of Alex. Who else? I love him to death, but sometimes his secretive nature makes me crazy. Have to wonder if Mrs. G is talking about her ex, Big Dave. "Only in my case, I *so* want to upset the balance. I'm ready to start throwing furniture around."

Mrs. G stares at me in surprise. "I've never known you to lose your temper."

"Don't worry. I won't set fire to your lovely outdoor setting here, Mrs. G. It's safe. Today anyway."

She laughs. "Maybe not. Might find me lobbing this chair into the neighbor's pool if you stick around long enough."

"You've had your super juice. I'm sure you'd have the strength," I say with a grin.

"Oh, that reminds me." She rises. "I meant to fix you another glass."

Standing, I put a hand on her arm. "Thanks, but I should get going. It's Friday night. You've probably got something planned, and I need to sort my bookshelves in accordance with the Dewey system."

"Believe me, your plans sound more exciting than mine." Mrs. G giggles as she walks me out to the front door. She leans on the doorjamb. "So tell me, how should I deal with this person who's frustrating me so much?"

Wide-eyed, I stare at her. "You're asking me?"

"Sure, Miss 5.0 GPA. I trust your opinion."

Shaking my head, I say, "I may have good grades, but I

still can't figure out what makes human beings tick. The best thing to do is tell them how the situation makes you feel and that you want to work together to make it better."

Mrs. G looks into the distance. "That's good advice. It's not putting blame on them. I like it. Really like it."

"I'll try it myself and let you know how it goes." I wrap her in a quick hug. Again, her bony ribs ring alarm bells inside me. "Please eat more. And I don't mean kale. Text me if you need anything."

"I will, Moll-Moll. Thanks," she whispers.

AS I TRUDGE along the sidewalk, guilt pings me. What I didn't say is that I *have* been trying to tell Alex how I feel about him throwing his life away, but he's not listening to a single syllable. Am I doing something wrong?

I've made plenty of mistakes. But nothing that couldn't be fixed. In my mind, there's a solution to everything. You've got to spend time figuring it out, that's all.

A car horn honks just before I reach the T-junction. Throwing an annoyed look to my right, I keep walking. The car follows me and honks again.

"Listen, jerk. Can't a person walk in peace?"

"No one walks in L.A. Get in," comes the swift reply. Alex grins from the passenger window of a newish black pickup that has dents and scratches in virtually every panel. "And who are you calling a jerk, anyway?"

My face burns, then I smile, "Sorry. Make that *delinquent*."

"Yep, that's me." Alex laughs. I peer at him. He looks pale. I really don't think the kale diet is doing him or his mother any favors. They need real, solid food. Maybe I should invite them over for dinner at my place.

"Hey, Miss Molly!" Kip shouts from the driver's seat.

"Hi, Kip." I can't muster up a smile for the guy at all.

"Where are you going?" Alex asks. "Do you need a ride?"

"Home, and no, thanks." I continue down Sycamore. Kip crawls alongside the curb.

Alex reaches an arm out, but he isn't close enough to touch me. "Katie Hansen's having a party at the cove tonight. Wanna come along? There'll be popcorn."

"Among other things," Kip chuckles.

"I'll bet," I say in a cool tone. Flipping my brown ponytail, I fib, "I'm busy. Suze is coming over and—"

"Oh, yeah, we bumped into Suze at the mall. She said she'll be there," Alex says.

Great. Fabulous. I tell one little white lie and it backfires. How do I get out of this one?

SIX

Alex

"You've gotta tell her, man," Kip insists.

"Nope."

"She'll hate you." He lies back on my floor and tosses a foam basketball up and down.

"But I'll be dead, and I won't give a flying fuck." I grab the basketball mid-throw and send it to the hoop on the back of my bedroom door. We didn't end up surfing. Once we got to the cove, I made the mistake of telling him what happened outside the biology lab. So he dragged me to the mall instead. He ate two burgers. I watched.

"Think about your life *before* you die, then. Both of you will be miserable. Do you really wanna spend your last days feeling like crap?"

Most people don't associate Kip—college dropout, sometime weed dealer, contender for title of Laziest Guy on Earth—as being the reasonable type. But he is. He doesn't let anybody see that side of himself. A lot of people, including Molly, think he's the classic juvenile delinquent.

When Kip and I first started hanging out at the cove, the only things we talked about were the surf and barometric pressure. Seriously. Then one morning, he pulled me out of the water when I had a blackout.

He saw some of my surgical scars. Like the one on my right shoulder blade, where the docs carved out a big-ass malignant mole. I got around to telling him about the cancer. He told me his twin sister died of leukemia years ago.

Her name was Caitlin.

Well, that hit me like a billion volts of lightning. She was the same Caitlin I met a long time ago when I did time in the kids' hospital. We were both being treated for cancer. Before Caitlin, I'd never had someone close to me die. I still think about her a lot.

Even more now I'm in the same canoe that she was in then. Sailing to the edge of a mile-high waterfall and knowing we're going to plunge right off. I don't know where *I'll* end up, but I'm pretty sure those angels Caitlin used to talk about swooped down and took her somewhere safe.

"No question, Kip. Near the end, I'm going to feel like crap, look like crap, probably say a lot of crap. Why would I want anyone to see me like that? Especially Molly. I don't want her to remember me as some broken-down wreck."

"Yeah, I get that." He stands and does bicep curls with my ten-pound dumbbells. I make a mental note to give those to him. Haven't lifted weights in months. "But you don't wanna be alone either."

"I can deal." I shove my biochemistry textbook hard into a bookcase. Pain jags down my arm. I wince and turn away.

The dumbbells thump on the rug. "Hey, are you all right? Want me to get your pain meds?"

Keeping my back turned, I say, "I took a couple of pills. It takes a while to kick in sometimes."

Not sometimes. Most of the time. Wasn't that long ago that all I needed was aspirin. Rarely at that. My doctors prescribed a bunch of medications to help numb me temporarily. What am I going to do when even the maximum dose won't kill the pain anymore?

Lowering my voice, I ask, "When are you getting me the stuff?"

Marijuana is legal in California if you're over eighteen. My eighteenth birthday is more than a year away, so, yeah, that's a problem for me. Even though Mom puts all her faith in the power of green vegetables and green fruit, she's not convinced about a particular green herb when it comes to pain relief. So she won't give her permission for me to try it, even under strict supervision.

Which leads me to Kip.

Surprisingly, he's as much of a roadblock as my mother, but for his own reasons.

"I told you, man. I really wanna help you. But I had to break my old connections. I'm trying to get clean. I *am* clean," he says. For the past few months he's been going to an AA-type of group for teens. I turn around and see turmoil written all over his face.

In the old days, Kip was in high demand, so to speak, at parties. Holding court in a dark corner of a basement or a backyard. Supplying weed. Molly and I never went near him. We wouldn't admit it to each other, but we were actually scared of him.

You can't help a dying man just once? I want to say now. But I get it. Mostly. I haven't got much to lose, unlike Kip. He's got his whole life ahead of him. The guy's made mistakes. Mistakes he doesn't want to repeat.

"There's bound to be a joint or two at this beach party," he says, sounding like he's trying to make it up to me.

"Yeah, true."

Kip checks his watch. "Let's get going."

My mother traps us at the bottom of the stairs. "Oh, good. I was about to call you down to see what you wanted for dinner."

"And we were about to head out to a party." I glance at the door, hardly able to look at her face. When I finally do, I see her lips are pressed together so tight they almost disappear. "But, um, we can stay for a snack. Right, Kip?"

"Sure, sounds great," he replies, giving my mom an angelic smile.

Later, having stuffed our faces with grilled cheese, chicken and—surprise!—kale sandwiches, Mom pulls me aside while Kip's in the bathroom. "I haven't had a chance to talk to you all day. I really don't want you to go out tonight. You *fainted* today."

"Mom, I'm all right. I feel good," I say. And I do. There's something magical about melted cheese. "I need to go to this party. It's on the beach. It'll make me feel alive."

Her eyes well up and she blinks rapidly. Turning, she says in a dejected voice, "I want you home at ten, okay? Not a minute later."

That's crazy. My usual curfew is eleven. "But—"

"That'll give you four hours. Plenty of time. It's the least you can do for missing your appointments."

Another round of guilt stirs inside me. It doesn't go so well with that gooey cheddar clogging my stomach. "Okay, okay."

"I've got an idea. Why don't I pick you up?"

"Why don't I catapult myself into the sun?"

"I get it. You're embarrassed by your own mother." She

digs into her purse and sticks a twenty-dollar bill in my hand. "Use that for a taxi in case you can't get a ride home."

"I'll get an Uber." I smirk. "Sounds like you don't exactly trust Kip. He's been a really good buddy to me, Mom."

She shrugs. "Yes, but I know how things work at these parties. Your ride hooks up with someone and the next thing you know, you're hitchhiking home."

"Yeah, maybe when you were young," I groan.

"Hey!"

Kip comes back to the kitchen and lifts his brows at me. "You ready?"

"Yep." Turning to Mom, I give her a quick hug. "Thanks for dinner. See you later."

"Have fun," she says faintly.

We head out to Kip's car. As I click my seatbelt on, I look up and see the living room lights dim. The silhouette of Mom's thin, lone figure is visible behind the curtains. More guilt sloshes inside me. What if that was the last conversation I ever had with my mom? A stupid semi-argument about curfews and hitchhiking?

I unsnap the seatbelt. "Hey, one second, okay?"

I don't even wait for Kip to reply. I run as fast as I can into the house. Mom's standing in front of the TV, studying the *Rebel Without a Cause* DVD cover. She looks up at me with wide eyes.

"Did you forget something?"

"Yeah." I cross the room in three big strides and scoop her into a rib-bruising hug.

She laughs. "What's gotten into you?"

What's gotten into me? A bunch of tumors and the thought of imminent death, that's all.

"Love you, Mom." I squeeze her one more time and then sprint back to the car.

———

BY THE TIME we get to the cove, what's left of the sun is a thin strip of orange and pink on the horizon. Still enough light around to see the faces in a group that gets bigger and bigger by the minute. Kip veers off to catch up with old buddies standing by the beginnings of a bonfire. Out of habit, I scan the crowd, looking for Molly. She's not big on parties, but maybe Suze convinced her to go. Then again, if Molly doesn't want to do something, it's hard to change her mind.

In a way, I'm glad she isn't here. There are a hundred different reasons why I can't be with her now, all of them very good. I let my shoulders relax and watch a couple of surfers ride one last set. Both seem to know what they're doing out there, but they're taking a risk. Twilight is not only happy hour for vampires. It's prime feeding time for sharks.

I kick my shoes off and head to the shoreline. Cold water laps my toes. I stare down at the froth easing over and back until I'm sort of hypnotized. I've eaten a lot of fish all my life. It'd be poetic justice if a great white snapped me up whole like a piece of sashimi. No more waiting around for the cancer to pick me off. Question is, am I brave enough to tempt a shark into taking me as a main meal? Stupid enough? A few months from now, will I be desperate enough?

Course not much goes to plan in my life. Sharks probably wouldn't come near me. The more likely scenario is I'll go out into the water after dark and the worst thing that'll hit me is a piece of slimy seaweed. Right in the kisser.

Then it'd be back to square one.

"Alex?" a voice calls out behind me. "Alex! Hey!"

Molly. Guess Suze has incredible powers of persuasion and managed to drag her here. Squeezing my eyes shut, I take a deep breath and steel myself. No way will Molly pass up a chance to hassle me about college and skipping school and God knows what else is on her mind. When I open my eyes again, she's right beside me, taking off her flip-flops.

"How are you?" she asks with so much concern I almost fall over. I expected anger from her. Maybe nostrils flaring in defiance and flashing, indignant eyes.

But not concern.

She's looking at me like I've got a "fragile" sticker on my forehead. I turn my gaze back on the surfers. They're paddling in, not far from the relative safety of dry sand.

"Me? I'm fine. Just thinkin' up ways to die," I say, partly to scare her off, but mostly because it's the truth.

"Morbid much?" She arches a brow. "What's on your list so far? Drowning? Getting hit by a boat propeller?"

"Look who's morbid now? Not to mention gruesome." I pretend to shiver. After a few beats, I tell her, "Shark attack. How would you rate that as a way to die?"

She frowns. "Apparently, sharks don't even like the taste of human flesh. That's why, in a lot of cases, people get a chunk taken out of them or a limb bitten off. Sharks take one bite and realize it's not a seal they're chowing down on and spit you out. You, of course, would know this if you'd—"

Bristling, I stop her. "I know what you're going to say. I'd know if I'd been in school."

"No," she says with a smirk. "You'd know about all that if you'd watched Shark Week."

I let out a laugh, grateful she's not hammering me about skipping classes for once. Lying to her about my impending doom is one of the hardest things I've ever had to do. The more we skate around the topic of school, the better.

Molly swishes her foot from side to side in the water. Music and excited voices float down the beach to us. The sun's all but gone now. We watch the two surfers finally climb out, looking exhausted but exhilarated at the same time. I know that feeling. I live for it.

Finally, Molly speaks up. "There's a, um, rumor going around about you."

My back stiffens. God. Somebody found out about the cancer? How? Kip wouldn't tell. I trust him. I try to focus on the sea, 'cause if I look at Molly, I'll crack. The winds are whipping up a little more. If only those surfer dudes had stayed in a few minutes longer. I work hard to keep my voice even. "Oh, yeah? Whatever it is, I didn't do it."

She steps closer to me. Her long silky hair brushes against my arm. "So you didn't faint in class today?"

Still trying not to look at her, I say, "No, I didn't faint in class."

That's not exactly a lie. I fainted *outside* the biology lab. In the hallway.

"Oh," she says simply. She looks a little more relieved, a little less concerned. "But you would tell me if something like that happened, right? We're still friends, aren't we?"

This time I turn to Molly. Wide-eyed, freckle-faced Molly, who has no idea how cute she really is. I don't even remember the exact moment I fell in love with her, but I can't imagine being *out* of love with her. Yet I don't want Molly to fall in love with *me*. Not when I've got a death sentence.

The words of Mom, of Kip, of my conscience echo

inside me. Tell her the truth. She deserves to know. She deserves the chance to prepare herself.

Would it be so bad if we made some good memories together before I get too sick, though? And then, when I can't hide the cancer from her any longer, I'll tell her. Everything.

"Moll, of course we're friends. That'll never change, no matter what." It takes every ounce of strength I've got to not blurt out the truth—that I want to be more than friends with her.

She looks at me sheepishly. "Even if I say I went ahead and reserved plane tickets to Connecticut? For spring break?"

"What?! I can't just get on a plane to visit colleges. Are you out of your mind?" I yell. She shrinks back in shock and immediately I feel stabs of guilt. She's probably thinking, *Well, why the hell not?* "I'm sorry. Sorry."

"Relax!" she shouts back. "The tickets are refundable."

Breathing deeply, I try to get a hold of my emotions again. "Good."

"And why is it good? You've always talked about going to Yale. This is your chance to see it for yourself. I wanted to get you inspired again."

Keep breathing, Alex. Keep breathing. Yeah, until you literally can't breathe anymore. Fighting for composure, I force myself to say, "Thanks, Moll. Really. But now's not the right time."

"I can change the reservations. How about May? The weather'll be fantastic."

I swallow hard. My body will not be fantastic three months out from death. Will it withstand a five-hour-plus flight? Nope. And for what, anyway? I'm not going to survive long enough to graduate from high school.

Tentatively, I put a hand on her shoulder. She jumps like she wasn't expecting me to touch her. "Molly, do me a favor?"

She brightens. "Anything. What do you need?"

Roaring, snarling engines tear my attention away from Molly for a second. They sound like they're closing in on the cove, ready to join the party.

"I need you to cancel the tickets." I start walking up the beach, sand squeaking between my wet toes. "I'm not going to Yale. Stop asking me why."

"Alex! ALEX!" she shouts after me. "You're an ass, you know that? And you can go jump in the ocean with a million rabid, hungry sharks for all I care!"

SEVEN

Molly

"I heard you scream at Alex. What happened?" Suze asks when I plunk beside her on a log. In front of us, the bonfire rages. Some kids are setting marshmallows on fire and running up and down the beach with flaming sticks.

My gaze sweeps over the partygoers. "Is he still here? I'm not actually done screaming at him."

She puts a hand on my arm. "Whoa there. Maybe you should cool off."

"Is he here?" I repeat crisply.

Suze sighs and jerks her thumb toward the parking lot. "A couple of seniors rocked up in their tricked-out cars. Alex went that way along with half the other boys to kick tires or get high on fumes or something."

A revving engine punctuates her words. I make a move to stand, but Suze pulls me down. "Hey! I was only going to get a drink."

"No, you weren't," she says, rolling her eyes. "You were

going on the hunt for Alex. Stay with me a while. You're my date tonight, remember?"

Heaving a sigh, I say, "Fine, but don't expect me to make out with you."

She throws her head back and laughs. "It's okay. I know you're saving yourself for someone else."

"What are you talking about?"

Suze offers me a chip, then digs into the bag. "Not what. Who. Alex. You've conveniently avoided admitting you like him."

"Is all that processed cheese affecting your brain?" I point at the Cheetos she's stuffing into her mouth.

"Stop lying to me. No, better yet, stop lying to yourself." Suze dusts off her hands. "You, my friend, should no longer deny your total, raging crush on Alex Gibson. You'll be a lot less grumpy if you just say it."

I squeak in protest.

"Don't pretend for my sake. My thing with Alex... Well, you can't even call it a thing because nothing happened between us. So don't even think of telling yourself he's off limits."

"Suze, you've got it all wrong—"

"Nope, not this time." She holds up an orange-stained palm. "Girl, if you want him, go after him!"

"But I don't want him!"

"Riiiight. You only talk about him 24/7."

I wince. So I'm a broken record. That must be beyond boring for everyone else. It's a wonder Suze sticks by me. "I'm not *that* bad, am I?"

With a laugh, she says, "You are that bad. But it's adorable. You two are adorable together, and you obviously care a lot about him."

I gaze at the crackling fire. The flames reach ever higher

toward the stars. "I don't want things to change between me and Alex."

"They won't have to. Well, some things will, and for the better." She nudges me. "I'm sure you'll have fun making out with *him*."

A strange feeling buzzes around my stomach. Kissing Alex. Feeling his arms around me. The thought of being close to him—physically—isn't that foreign. Or as gross as the thought of kissing Jared Christie over there chugging beer. It's pretty clear to anyone who gets close to Jared that he doesn't brush his teeth and often wears the same T-shirt two weeks running.

No, Alex has got the personal hygiene thing down pat. That's a plus. And he's got a nice smile. I always feel like he could brighten the gloomiest day with that wide grin. And the way he fixes broken gadgets and gifts them to me is completely awesome and thoughtful.

"You shouldn't let him get away," Suze says, echoing what I'm thinking at the same time.

Then my chest deflates. "I don't want him to, but there's one problem. He's had it with me interfering in his life."

"He said that to you?"

"Not in so many words, but he's pulling back from me. Maybe I've been too obsessed with the college thing and it's scared him off." I glance over at the cars. A group of kids moves and finally I spot Alex and Kip. They're running their hands over a black Porsche like it's a thoroughbred horse. "Plus, I've pretty much told him he's dead to me, so I don't think it's meant to be. Not romantically, anyway."

Suze shrugs. "Apologize to him. Then see where things go."

"Oh, and he'll forgive me just like that?" I click my fingers.

Holding out her hand, she says, "Fifty bucks says he will."

"You're on." I shake on it, then fold my arms and stare at the fire till my vision goes blurry. I can't help but think Alex is the one who owes *me* an apology for being a general jerk during the past few months.

She lightly shoves me off the log. "No, lady. *You're* on."

"What?" I scramble to my feet.

"I mean, the spotlight's on you. Get up there and make things right between you and your soon-to-be-boyfriend."

"Let's take one step at a time. We need to just be friends again." I frown and shake sand off my skinny jeans. "I cannot believe you pushed me."

"You're welcome," she singsongs, batting her long eyelashes.

I pull her up. "And you're coming with me."

"Fine, fine." She stashes the Cheetos into her purse and links arms with me.

We trudge past clusters of seniors and juniors from school, including the birthday girl, Katie.

"Don't go!" Katie leans toward us. Her eyes are glazed and round like doughnuts. She points to a cooler at her feet. "Party's just starting."

"We'll be right back," Suze calls out as we pass. "With boys!"

"For my birthday?" Katie slurs and grins. "You two are the best!"

We step off the cool sand onto hot asphalt. Kids are swarming around cars, whooping every time a car engine revs. The smell of rich gas and burning rubber competes with the fresh air.

"Why does this turn guys on?" I ask, fanning my nose.

"They're weirdos from Mars." Suze tugs my arm.

"Come on, I see Kip and Alex. Oh, look. They're talking to Tom. We can bring him to Katie later."

I saw them from a mile off, too, but I wanted to take my time getting closer. What the hell am I going to say to Alex? Is he even going to hear me apologize over these obnoxious engine noises?

I take a couple of steps, then stop dead. "Are you implying you want Kip for yourself? *Kip?*"

Under the solar-powered parking lot lights, Suze's blush is plain to see. "I mean, Katie can choose between Tom and Kip."

Rolling my eyes, I continue walking. What is it with this Kip guy? Why is he so magnetic to everyone but me?

Alex turns his head and meets my gaze. I falter. And so does Alex's smile. He turns back to Tom.

"Come on," Suze mutters. "You can be the bigger person here. Apologize. Tell him he's the best thing that ever happened to you and kiss him senseless."

"Do I have to do that in front of you? And everyone?"

"Maybe only me, so I know you've successfully carried out your mission." She winks and propels me forward.

"So what do you say?" Kip is asking Tom when we reach them. "A little street race for my boy here?"

Tom leans against his gleaming, black, and very expensive Porsche. A little something his movie producer parents gave him for his eighteenth birthday. It was a replacement for the BMW sedan he'd gotten for his sweet—ha!—sixteenth. Both cars cost more than all the contents of my house. In our school, there's a big gap between the haves and have-nots. It must be hard for Alex, who fell swiftly into the have-not group when his parents divorced after the longest separation in history.

"I don't know..."

"It's for a good cause," Kip cajoles. Alex stands by the car, looking like a kid in a chocolate factory.

"Which good cause is that?" I ask, walking up behind Kip.

He jumps.

Tom angles toward me and Suze. "Hey. How you doing? Long time no talk, Suze."

Studiously ignoring Kip, she replies, "Oh, you know, been busy. Nice wheels."

He grins. "Kip's trying to convince me to let Alex drive it."

"Why?" I ask warily, thinking of James Dean and the way he drove fast and died young. In a freakin' Porsche.

Alex shrugs without looking at me. "YOLO."

I turn to Tom. "You're not seriously thinking of giving him the keys, are you?"

Tom scratches the back of his neck. He rakes his gaze over the car. To me, it looks like a coiled rattlesnake ready to strike. "Well, I know Alex is pretty cautious. He tutored me in calculus."

"Um, math and Porsches are two different beasts," I point out. "Formulas and equations are predictable if you know your way around them. Alex, you don't know your way around a car like this."

Alex finally looks at me. "Did somebody call the fun police?"

His words are like poison ivy, making me itch like crazy. I am not going to be making out with Alex Gibson tonight. No way.

"Playing NASCAR games on your PlayStation does not count as real driving experience," I insist. *James Dean. Car crash. Porsche. Dead.* Those words keep jumbling up in my brain. If Alex gets behind the wheel and wraps that car around a streetlight, I'll never forgive myself.

"Hey, come on, Miss Molly, that's all the more reason to try the real deal," Kip speaks up. "Stop busting his ass all the time."

Steam practically vents out of my ears. "I'm not busting his ass! I'm looking out for him."

"And so am I!" Kip takes a couple of steps closer to me.

Suze grips my arm tightly. She whispers, "We should get out of here. This is all getting a little wild."

I stand my ground.

"Kip, don't," Alex warns.

"But Miss Molly, you're so busy thinking about yourself that you can't see Alex is—"

"Kip!" Alex moves between me and Kip, whose eyes are getting wilder by the second. And scarier. But I will not be intimidated by that loser. Judging by the way Alex is glaring, standing over him, maybe he finally gets it. Kip is bad news.

Kip peers around at me and starts waving his arms. "Alex is—"

"No!" Alex roars. He grabs Kip by the collar and throws him against the Porsche's driver's side.

"Hey, hey, watch it!" Tom pulls Kip away from the shiny paintwork. He lovingly inspects the undamaged door. "You know what? I'm gonna leave you guys to it. I'll take you for a ride some other time, Alex."

Tom gets into the Porsche. He theatrically guns the engine and makes the tires spin before peeling away in the direction of Malibu. The four of us left behind choke on the thick stench of burning rubber.

Kip shoots a look at me. He opens his mouth like he's going to say something terrible.

Alex glares at Kip. In a menacing tone, he says, "Not one word."

Shaking his head violently, Kip swings around toward me. "I used to think you were good for Alex. Not so much now."

"Alex and I have been friends since we were four. I know him better than anyone!" My chest puffs indignantly. I cannot be*lieve* I'm having this conversation with Kip Jones, of all people. "What gives you the right to pass judgment on me? You don't even know me or Alex."

Kip settles down a little. He looks at the ground, hands on hips. "I know more than you think."

Putting a hand on Kip's shoulder, Alex practically begs, "Don't say anything else, man. How many times do I have to tell you? I'll do this my way."

His voice is low. I'm sure he didn't mean for me to hear. Do *what* his way?

"This is getting boring. Let's go back to the party." Suze tugs on my arm again. I know she's not being superficial, though. She's trying to be a good friend, trying to steer me back to the relative safety of the beach.

Like a bad friend, I ignore her. I stare first at Kip, then at Alex. There's an undercurrent between them. It's palpable, pulsating. Something is *definitely* up. "What's going on? You're both acting weird."

"Nothing." It seems to take a lot of effort, a lot of control, for Alex to utter that one word. He won't take his eyes off Kip.

"Tell her." Kip's jaw clenches. "Or I will."

Alex turns into a statue. Immobile. Unable to talk. He won't meet my gaze, but he keeps staring hard at Kip.

Suze lets out an enormous, annoyed sigh. "You two are

the worst drama queens ever. I'm here to have fun. Moll, are you coming?"

"No, I'm staying right here." Something deep inside warns me that I need to be around for Alex. Who knows what Kip's capable of?

"You have no right to tell her, Kip," Alex says. "Just like you had no right to tell Tom. You don't get to do that."

"Will one of you, I don't care *who*, tell me what the hell is happening here?" My voice carries over the revving of engines. I feel the weight of a dozen gazes on me. Kip shifts from foot to foot, and looks up at the sky. His lips purse.

Slowly, Alex swivels to me. Clearing his throat, he says, "Molly, come with me."

"Where?" I whisper. The cold feeling returns as he shakes his head. I throw a glance at Suze, who looks confused and scared.

Alex takes my hand and leads us away from the glare of the parking lot lights, away from the stares. It's strange to feel his palm against mine. Warm and firm. At the same time, it feels right. Natural. Calming. Some of the coldness inside me goes away.

But I'm still worried. "Alex, I can't wait anymore. Please talk to me."

"Everything's going to be fine," he says in a reassuring voice.

A three-quarter moon sheds enough light for us to see the path ahead. Alex takes me along the top of the beach, then down to the jagged edges of the cove. His hand grips tighter as he approaches a flat boulder overlooking the sea. We sit side by side. Salt water sprays our faces, cooling us down.

"You want to know the truth?" he asks.

"No, go ahead. Tell me more lies."

He laughs. It's a rough, weary sound. "You're right. I have been lying to you."

My spine goes rigid. It's hard to hear those words come out of his mouth. We've always confided in each other. Till very recently. Now I know for sure he's been avoiding me. Lying to me. "What about?"

"Everything. My life." Alex swallows hard. He stares into the distance. A line of oil tankers inches across the horizon, lights blazing. "I'm going to lose you."

"Why would you think that? Because you've told a few lies? I'm not *that* unforgiving."

"It's not that." He shakes his head. "I'm... leaving."

"Are you moving to Australia to be with your dad?" I whisper, my insides churning. I miss him already, and he's right here with me. "It's not for forever, though, is it? You *have* to come back, because Yale's going to accept you in a heartbeat."

"Molly, I'm sorry." He grabs both my hands and squeezes like we're riding ten-foot ocean waves together and can't get separated. "What I said about living fast, dying young..."

"Yeah." I ignored it till now, but an intense fear is making my bones shake. It's the way he says the word *dying* that makes me feel the worst pain.

"I may not be living all that fast." He strokes my hand with his trembling thumb. "But I'm gonna die young. For real."

"What?" I stare at him uncomprehendingly, unable to move.

"Molly?"

"No." Tears blur my vision. "It's not true."

His voice cracks. "Molly, I have stage IV melanoma. I'm dying."

"Stop it. Don't joke about it." *Not true. Not true. Not true.* He's beaten cancer once, when he was a little kid. Now he's bigger and stronger. He's invincible, dammit.

My heart and my mind start to make the connections. Missing school. Losing hair. Losing weight. Losing interest in the future.

Oh, God. How could I have been so blind? What kind of best friend am I?

I put an arm around him. Try to weld myself to him.

"I'm not joking, Molly." He shudders as he breathes deeply. Connected by his touch, I shudder along with him. It's like the earth's shattering beneath us. Cracking wide open. Ready to swallow us whole. "I'm dying. And there's nothing anyone can do about it. Not even you."

EIGHT

Alex

"No!" Molly gasps as if she took a direct hit from a sledgehammer. A tidal wave of tears spills over her lashes. Seated on the boulder, she wobbles sideways. I reach out to bring her back to me, but she pushes against my chest. "You're lying. If you're not joking about it, you're lying. Again."

"Trust me, I wouldn't lie or joke about something like this. Not to you." I clench my fists, partly to stop myself from touching her again. "But God knows I lied to myself. Tried to tell myself it wasn't happening."

She draws in a shaky breath. "I won't let you die."

"It doesn't work that way," I say, shaking my head. "Death doesn't bend to Molly Corbett's wishes."

Her voice pitches higher. "And what about Alex Gibson's wishes?"

"My wishes? There are so many I can't prioritize them anymore. And none are ever going to come true." I bite down on my lip. The salty sea taste is a welcome change after weeks of subsisting on Mom's bitter kale smoothies.

"Oh, my God," she breathes. "You've given up. That's why you haven't been going to school and why you've been avoiding college applications."

"Well, Molly, you tell me," I snap. "If you were given six months to live, would you want to spend it cramming for pointless exams and being forced to attend pep rallies?"

Her jaw goes slack. "Six months? That's all?"

"Okay, five months and twenty-seven days. Give or take."

She doesn't smile at my attempt at a joke. Even in the weak light, the hurt on her face is easy to see. "Why didn't you tell me? When did you find out?"

I look away. "Last year. When I was in Sydney visiting Dad."

Molly lets out a sob and struggles to compose herself. "I don't understand how this happened. How you could have cancer a second time. It's so unfair!"

It was sort of easier finding out when I was half a world away. Easier to hide the news from Molly, that is. It gave me time to clear my head. When the doctors told us the rounds of chemo hadn't worked and there's nothing else they could do, my head got completely clogged again.

"My dad has had a few skin cancers cut out over the years," I say, trying to keep my voice from shaking. "Growing up by the beach in Australia, he worshipped the sun, you know? And I wanted to do everything he did. Stayed out on the waves from dawn till dusk if I could. Ignored my mother when she lectured me about using sunblock and all the rest of it.

"Anyway, I went along with Dad for one of his regular check-ups. A nurse at the clinic didn't like the look of a mole on my neck. I got a biopsy right away. The rest is history." I breathe in sharply. "You should have seen my dad's face when the docs gave us the diagnosis. He looked so guilty. But I don't blame him for anything. He gave me the love of surfing. I never feel more alive than when I'm out there on my board."

Or when I'm with you.

Molly weeps silently. "I'm so sorry I wasn't there for you, Alex."

Shrugging, I say, "There's nothing to apologize for. My parents went into full-on Papa Bear and Mama Bear mode. Did everything they could to get me the best treatment. Meanwhile, I was numb. Just a piece of driftwood getting tossed around. I went in whatever direction they told me to go. Even if you were there, I don't think it would've been good for you to be near me."

"But that's ridiculous!"

"Not really," I tell her. "A counselor talked to me about grief and loss. You know how they talk about those stages? Denial, anger, bargaining, depression, acceptance. I didn't want you to see how angry I was."

"And your new buddy Kip? When did you tell him?" There's a shade of accusation in her voice. Envy and pain, too.

"Look, I know now I should have told you, but at the time, I didn't know the right way to deal with all this."

After a while, she says quietly, "I don't know if there is a right way."

"I'm sorry Kip found out before you did. It happened by accident." I tell her about my blackout here at the cove and the connection to Kip's sister Caitlin.

"Wow. That's... that's amazing. I'm sorry. I didn't mean to get all bent out of shape about who knew first. I can't believe this is happening!" Her gaze drops to her fidgeting hands. "Were you ever going to tell anyone?"

I sigh. "I had this grand plan to fade away without anyone knowing."

"What, and not allow anyone to say goodbye?" There's that accusing tone again.

"Yep. No funeral, no memorial. It's not like I've done anything important in my sixteen or so years on the planet."

Molly gives me a doubtful look. "You've been my best friend since forever. Always bringing me gadgets and making me laugh. I think that's pretty darn important."

I squeeze her hand as hard as I can. "Hey, you've been my BFF. You *are* my best friend."

Best friend. What would it be like if I kissed my best friend now? Kissed her like I've wanted to since our first day as Palisades High freshmen? I'd been away all summer and instead of coming home to tomboy Molly, I found grown-up Molly with curves in places that weren't there before.

Molly eyes me thoughtfully. Is she thinking what I'm thinking? Will she ever dream of kissing me, knowing I'm going to die anyway?

"What stage of grief are you at now?" she asks.

My shoulders slump. I guess kissing is the last thing on her mind.

"I'm at the unofficial 'I don't give a shit' stage. But sometimes I go through *all* of those other stages in the course of an hour." I look over at the ocean. White-capped waves roll one after the other. The sea has been the one constant thing my whole life. Whether here in L.A. or in Sydney, I've never lived more than a few blocks away from it. "There'll come a day when I won't be able to grab my board and paddle out. And I'm okay with that. Today, anyway."

Her gaze rakes over me, lingering on my chest. "But you look so good."

"Stop it. You're making me blush," I say in a flat voice.

"I mean it. Apart from being kinda pale, you still look fit and muscly." Her voice trails off. She stares at my biceps. They're covered by my sleeves, but anyone can tell they're not as bulgy as they were at the start of the year. And that really blows because I worked so hard to build those suckers up.

"Must be the smoothies Mom makes for me. I'm surprised my skin isn't green right now."

"Alex, listen." Molly jiggles my arm. "We can fight this with kale, with positivity, proactivity, hyperactivity! You beat lymphoma, for God's sake. You can beat this, too."

Numbly, I stare into her eyes. In the moonlight, they're dark and stormy instead of their usual calm green. "Yeah, I did beat cancer the first time around, but the odds are not in my favor now."

"Who says?" Her tone's defiant. She really is not going take this sitting down.

And I can't blame her. I felt the same way. Once.

"Because I've had second, third, fourth and fifth opinions!"

"Then get a sixth one," she says, exasperated.

Despite everything, I smile. "Find one for me, and I'll go."

"Okay, then." Molly pulls out her phone and starts googling.

"I didn't mean right now." I chuckle. "Are you for real?"

"Yes, I'm for real! We're talking life and death. There isn't a second to waste." She yelps when I rip the phone from her grip and toss it safely aside on a patch of sand.

"Let's chill here now and come up with a list tomorrow." I say the words, but secretly I hope she'll forget them in the morning. Soon she'll understand that *terminal* really does mean *beyond hope*. Besides, we've gone to the very best oncologists we could find. They all pretty much said I'm doomed.

"How do they even come up with that deadline?" She stops and winces at how literal her words are. "I mean, does anyone *really* know?"

"If I'm still alive and kicking after six months and one day, you get to come over and badger me about not sticking to timetables."

Darkly, she says, "Do not even kid around with me right now."

I swing my leg over the boulder. "I don't know what else to do anymore except make stupid jokes."

After a few minutes of thinking, she says, "You know what you've got to do now, right?"

"What?" I say uneasily.

"Make every word, every action, every second count."

"Does that mean I have to stay awake 24/7 for the next six months? Can I at least get a siesta in the afternoons?"

She doesn't even crack a smile. I hope she gets her sense of humor back soon. She'll need it.

"No, it means we are going to carry on as if you haven't been given six months to live."

I stare at her, dismayed. Didn't I tell her bluntly that I'm a dead man walking? Maybe joking about death isn't such a good idea after all.

Molly goes on. "What if the five or six doctors are all wrong? What if you defy the odds and survive? Where will that leave you?"

"You're saying I should pretend everything's hunky dory and keep going to school? I've already told you, the

Yale dream has crashed and burned. Why would I even want to apply? I'd be wasting everyone's time. Plus, I might be in the way of someone who really deserves to be there."

"*You* deserve to be there. We'll research drug trials," she insists, clearly not listening to a thing I'm saying. "What if someone finds a cure or—"

"Don't you get it?" I cut her off. "There's no future for me. No miracle cure. Nothing."

"You've still got a future that's at least six months long," Molly mutters. She squeezes her eyes shut. When she opens them again, she looks determined. "I'll take six months off, too."

"No! You can't put your life on hold for me." I'm floored. She'd seriously do that?

Looking defiant, she lifts her chin. "What's six months when I have to face the rest of my life without you?"

NINE

Molly

I watch Alex jog from his front door toward my car parked alongside the curb. My brain still can't process what's happening. How is it possible that my best friend is *dying?* It can't be true. But Mrs. G confirmed it, admitted all those pill bottles were for Alex and not for managing her menopause. A part of me aches because Alex didn't tell me about the cancer sooner. I know where he was coming from now. I'm just not sure I'd handle things the same way if I were in his sneakers.

"Welcome to T-minus seventy-nine days," Alex says cheerfully, strapping himself into the passenger seat.

"Ugh, do you have to say that?"

"Yep. My last words will be *blast-off!*"

On cue, I fire the engine. I came through on my threat to take a leave of absence from school. With parental blessing, of course. How could they or the school admin refuse my perfectly reasonable request to help take care of a dying friend? When I'm not spending as much time as possible with Alex, I'll have to continue my schoolwork at home. Small price to pay.

"What are we doing today?" I press a button to wind down his window. In a robotic, GPS-lady voice, I continue, "I'm awaiting your instruction. Just tell me the coordinates. Or a rough address."

Alex laughs and rests his elbow on the windowsill. "I hadn't really thought this thing through when I texted you last night. We could go cruising."

Concentrating on the thickening traffic near the beach, I suggest, "How about a road trip? I hear there's a quaint little university about three thousand miles away that you might want to see."

"Isn't it enough that I wrote the essay you've been bugging me about?"

I smile. "Not quite. Next step is to actually send it."

"Sure. You know I'm signing it off with Alexander 'Six-Feet-Under-By-the-Time-You-Read-This'   Gibson, right?"

"Alex!" *He* may be deep in the acceptance stage of grief, but I'm still wallowing in the denial phase.

"What's your problem? It's full disclosure."

"You *might* be gone," I growl. "There's always hope."

"We'll see," he mutters. Further down the PCH, he points to Burger Deluxe. "I'd kill for any type of food that isn't green right now. Are you hungry? My treat."

"This must be the shortest cruise in history. We haven't even seen a single girl for you to hit on."

"No girl will want me now." Before I can protest, he adds, "Besides, we haven't got a second to lose. Isn't that what you said? Let's do everything in double-time."

Quick as a flash, I find a parking spot, and we soon have steaming coffee and breakfast sitting in front of us. There's nothing green or anything else that resembles a vegetable on either of our plates.

I dress my pancakes with maple syrup and swirl it into the whipped cream. Alex jabs at his bacon, but leaves it sitting on the plate. There's a definite change in mood. Mouth full, I mumble, "Why aren't you eating?"

He winces at his mountain of scrambled eggs, hash browns and crispy bacon strips. It all looks and smells so good. "I'm not hungry anymore."

My fork freezes halfway to my mouth. I'm suddenly reminded that he's sick. He's dying. People lose their appetites when they're close to death, don't they? Tears start to well. Impossible to think I have any left. I wore out my tear ducts that night at the cove when Alex told me everything. "What's wrong? Are you in pain?"

He shakes his head like he's trying to remove something lodged in his brain. "I didn't mean to put a downer on breakfast. It's just that I feel fine a lot of the time. Then suddenly it hits me. When I'm trying to sleep. Brushing my teeth. Sitting in class. I'm fucking *dying*."

Fighting tears, I reach across our booth's table and lightly cover his hand with mine. "It's okay. Listen, I don't want you to hide anything from me ever again."

Alex stares at my hand. Finally, he lifts his hazel gaze and gives me an intense look. Two spots of red glow on his cheeks. "I can't promise you that. There are some things I don't want you or anybody else to know."

"Oh." Removing my hand, I sit back and breathe in deeply. My heart feels like it's shattering into a million tiny pieces. I tell myself he's totally within his rights to keep to himself. It's his life. His death. "Alex, are you scared?"

He looks out the spotless plate-glass window. Discarded fast-food wrappers roll among the parked cars. Tumbleweeds of the city. "See, if I were scared, that's definitely something I'd hide from you."

Peering at him, I find fear etched over every square inch of his face. "I'm guessing it's normal to feel scared in this situation."

"How would you know?" he snaps.

Refusing to flinch, I say in a calm voice, "I don't. I need you to tell me."

"There's nothing normal about what I'm going through," he says through grit teeth.

"You're right."

"I haven't *lived* yet." He takes two long gulps of coffee. I notice a faint tremor in his hand. He follows my line of vision and plunks down the sturdy cup. "And I'm only going to get weaker from here on out."

Pushing aside my plate, I take hold of his hands. Firmly this time. He doesn't squirm away. Maybe, I note with a marble-size lump in my throat, he doesn't have the strength. "Okay, I've been thinking about this 'live fast, die young' mantra."

He lifts an eyebrow. "Yeah?"

"We should totally do it. Live fast."

"We?"

"Yep, tell me what's on your bucket list and we'll strike each item off. One by one. Starting now." I let go of him and check my imaginary wristwatch. I press its imaginary button.

"But what if..." he lowers his voice and gives me a loaded look. "I want to do dangerous things?"

"Define 'dangerous.'"

Seemingly speechless, his mouth flaps open and closed. "Dangerous things are the kinds of things that make me *feel* something, you know?"

"Wow. So specific." I pour another sachet of sugar into my coffee.

"You're making fun of a dying man?" He gives a bitter-sweet smile.

"Hey, I'm not going easy on you now. No more feeling sorry for yourself." I'm carrying enough pain and pity inside to last two lifetimes. With my fingernail, I tap his phone screen. "Type five things you've never done before but have always wanted to try."

"Do they have to be legal things?"

"That's up to you," I say. "But if you need to be bailed out, I'll have to sell your car, my iPad and every other gadget you've given me so I can raise the cash."

Alex taps and swipes on his phone. "Do I have to tell you what these things are in advance?"

"That's also up to you."

His lips twist thoughtfully. "So, I can surprise you. Even though you hate surprises."

"When did I ever say I hate surprises?"

"Come on, Moll." He snorts. "You organize your life right down to the minute, allowing for every contingency. I got you good once, though. Remember your fifteenth birthday? *You* threw a tantrum when *I* threw a surprise party for you."

"How could I forget? You told me to come over for a study session. I turned up in mismatched sneakers and a rat's nest for hair. Plus, I had ketchup stains on my unicorn T-shirt."

"And a smear on your cheek. Can't forget that. You looked cute, though." He laughs, then stops abruptly.

"Cute?" Alex thought I looked cute? My stomach does a weird little jump. Somehow. I press a hand on my chest. Maybe I scarfed down those pancakes too fast. Or maybe it's a reaction to hearing Alex say I once looked cute—the same Alex who never comments about my appearance unless I'm red from heatstroke or green from eating bad shrimp.

"In... in a Little Rascals kind of way," he stammers. "Okay, I'll shut up now."

"No, please, do keep telling me how cute I used to be."

"Used to—" He breaks off. I throw the empty sugar packet at him. "Stop throwing things at me so I can write this bucket list before I actually kick the bucket."

Sitting back, I watch him tap with those long, lean fingers. He bites his bottom lip, deep in concentration. While he's busy, I swipe some of his bacon. He doesn't even blink. Finally, he puts his phone screen-side down on the table.

"You've finished your list?"

He grins enigmatically and fishes bills from his wallet. "You've finished my breakfast?"

I smack my lips. "The bacon was divine."

"Glad to hear it. Give me your car keys. Let's go."

TEN

Alex

A pack of cyclists zooms by us on the trail. Dust whirls after them and kicks up into our faces. Apart from that, it's a clear morning. In the distance, the stark white walls and dull copper domes of Griffith Park Observatory stand out.

I glance over at Molly. She's trying to balance on a rented mountain bike while pushing dark bangs away from her eyes. The bike's front wheel wobbles as she fights for control. It's an uphill battle. Literally.

"Maybe we should stick to the newbie trail," she says. "This one is for experts and show ponies."

"Nah, not dangerous enough." I try to control my breath. My lungs are close to bursting. We're supposedly on the intermediate trail. But for someone who hasn't ridden a bike since middle school, even the gentle slopes here seem like death traps. I know it must kill Molly to not be in charge of this excursion. She'd find the paths of least resistance, paths that didn't have razor-sharp bushes and bone-jarring ruts.

"Are we close to the top yet?" Molly pants. Sweat pours down her forehead. Her face is as red as Mars. And still she looks beautiful.

She would hate to know her face is an open book. Every emotion, every feeling, shows in those huge eyes. I could tell it shocked her when I said she was cute. It's something I've always thought, but never said out loud. Question is, do I have the guts to say it to her again? Molly didn't exactly fall at my feet. She only had eyes for the bacon.

"Less than a mile," I call out. "Piece of cake. You can do it!"

She flicks a look at me, then gives a firm nod. I know what she's thinking: If a half-dead guy like me can ride this trail, she can do a half-mile, too. Her short legs pump a little bit faster. "Come on, Alexander the Geek! Double-time!"

Within minutes, we're at the top of a ridge amongst groups of tourists, looking out across the L.A. basin. A bit of the marine layer clings near the horizon. Otherwise, the sky is wide and clear blue. Right in front of us, the Hollywood sign stretches out across a hill.

"Wow," Molly says simply. She shares her bottle of water with me. "I've lived here all my life and have *never* seen the sign up close."

"Same." I grin at her and pull out my phone. Molly has no clue that I'm taking shots of her as well as the sign.

Before, I thought it was weird that out-of-towners put this at the top of their sightseeing list—stare at a friggin' sign made of ordinary steel. Now, I wish *I* had more hours and days to take in those giant white letters.

We spend a while mixing around with the tourists and taking selfies. Molly subtly tries to find places in the shade where we can get a good view.

"Ready for the best part, Mollywood?" I drag her away from yet another vantage point.

Hope springs into her eyes. "What, are we going to climb the sign?"

I make an obnoxious buzzing noise, the kind heard on game shows. "Nope. We're going on a race to the bottom. Bonus points if you go hands-free for at least ten consecutive seconds."

She gives me a double high-five. "Let's do it."

Molly gets a head start on me. But, thanks to her shortage of coordination, almost immediately loses ground. Her left foot slips from the pedal, and it takes a few spins of the wheel to get resettled. I zoom past her, whooping triumphantly. The breeze whips my skin, but in a good way. I don't even mind the heat of the sun on my face or the effect of the bumpy terrain on my butt.

"Hey, Alex?" Molly calls out behind me. Her voice vibrates. "I think we took a wrong turn."

"What makes you say that?" I yell back.

"Look down to your left. See that smooth path everyone else but us is riding?"

My seat judders under me. I glance further ahead and spy deep ruts in the worn asphalt. I could avoid them. If I'm careful.

"Alex, we should turn back."

Over the rush of wind, I hear her tires skid on gravel. Alarmed, I throw a quick look over my shoulder. She's okay. Just standing with the bike stationary between her legs. And looking furious.

"Alex! Stop!"

I face the trail in front of me. Brambles whack my legs, but I don't care. My heart bashes against my ribs. Maybe it's the heat. Maybe the bumpy track's damaging my brain. But something tells me to keep going. Keep daring myself.

Molly's voice is far, far away.

I shut her out. Words from the past echo through my head.

"You're such a brave kid."

"What a trouper!"

"I know it hurts, but you've gotta be brave for your mom now."

Tears stream from my eyes. I want to think they're caused by wind blasting my eyeballs, but of course that's not exactly true.

"Come on, Alex," I bite out. "Let's see how fucking brave you are."

I pedal faster and faster. The harder I ride, the harder it is to control the front wheel. I wrench the bike left and right in order to stay on the trail.

"Alex!" Molly's voice is shrill and clear in my ear now. Did she catch up to me?

I turn my head slightly, and I catch sight of the sharp drop next to me. It's got to be fifty feet down into the canyon at least. My wheels spin inches away from the edge. One wrong move and I could go right over. Break my neck. Die.

It'd be so easy.

Chest pounding, I adjust my grip on the handlebars. The rhythm of the bike and the blur of the landscape put me into a trance.

And Molly's screams take me right out of it. "Alex! Are you trying to kill yourself?"

I squeeze the brake levers. The back wheel fishtails over the edge, but the rest of the bike—and my body—stays on the trail.

Panting, I turn to Molly. She's on foot, her bike nowhere to be seen. Wouldn't be surprised if she tossed it off the cliff. "Yeah. And so what if I am? It doesn't matter."

She stomps up to me and puts her hot palms on my shoulders. "It matters to me. *You* matter to me. You are not going to die. Not on my watch."

ELEVEN

Molly

There's one thing I've never, ever told Alex, and that is I hate swimming in the ocean. Pools I can handle. A calm lake is fine. But to me, the sea is an untamed, unchained animal. The idea of being caught in a riptide and dragged into the middle of the Pacific is nothing short of terrifying.

Surfing has always been Alex's thing. Just like going vintage clothes shopping has always been my thing. I couldn't care less if he knocks back a chance to try on seventies bellbottom jeans with me.

But I know he'll care very much if I back out of a surfing lesson.

Touching my head self-consciously, I step out of the cove's public restrooms. The short-sleeved, thigh-length wetsuit Alex bought me clings in all the wrong places. Now that the sun's on the move above the horizon, people will actually see me wearing this get-up. Not only do I feel like a seal, I look like one, too.

"Hey, you made it!" Alex calls out and jogs toward me.

For the first time, I notice he's acquired a limp. I hope to God he isn't in pain. But if I know Alex, he wouldn't want me to make a big deal out of it. Pushing away dark thoughts, I wave, then gesture at my back. "Help. I can't reach the zipper."

"Sure." When he reaches me, his sunny expression fades. "Whoa. What happened to your hair?"

"Attack of the stylist. She chopped twelve inches of hair. It's called a pixie cut. What do you think?" Channeling a catwalk model, I put a hand on my hip and show off an exaggerated pout.

"Pixie, huh?" He studies me for several long seconds. "You look like a little fairy penguin in that wetsuit."

I push his shoulder. Gently. Because that limp of his worries me.

His voice roughens. "I like it. Suits your face."

"High praise coming from you." I laugh.

"So what's with the big makeover?"

Trying to keep my tone light, I say, "I figured I had plenty of hair to share around."

His eyes bulge. "You donated your hair to charity?"

"Uh-uh. I found a company in Orange County that makes wigs for chemo patients." Tears begin to sting my eyes. I blink them away and quickly change the subject. "Can you zip me up now? I'm getting a chill here."

Alex spins me around. One hand curves around my neck, bringing warmth to the bare skin right there. He zips the last couple of inches and spins me again.

"So this is T-minus seventy-eight." Grandly, he sweeps his arm toward the beach. In the distance, a couple of surfer dudes sit up on their boards watching the sunrise. "Good thing we're here early, 'cause we've got a lot to do today. Starting with teaching you how to surf."

"Um, fabulous." I want to say I'm scared and want to go back to bed, but I bite my tongue. This isn't about me. And, really, I'm happy we're here. Alex said the ocean makes him feel alive. Yesterday, on the bike trail, he was *this* close to launching himself off a cliff. The longer we stay around the water, the safer he'll be.

Overnight, he'd somehow found a board that was the right size for me. And the right color—cobalt blue. The leg rope drags on the ground behind me as I follow Alex. Halfway to the shore, he drops his board on the sand, fins down.

"Okay, best place to learn how to surf is not out there." He points at the Pacific. A low swell rolls toward the shore. Then he points at the white sand under our toes. "It's here."

"Fine by me!" I say cheerfully.

Alex gives me a funny look. "Don't worry. As soon as you get your technique right, we're heading out."

I gulp and avoid looking at the waves.

"I'll demonstrate first." He jumps down. It might be my imagination, but *his* wetsuit isn't as clingy as mine. He's lost more weight than I realized. "Float your board on the water, then climb onto it on your stomach. Paddle, paddle, paddle with your arms. Head out past the breakers. Hang out with your buddies until a worthy set comes along. Angle your board to the beach, let the wave's momentum push you." He pauses. "You look spaced out. Are you getting all this?"

"Yep, keep going." The only thing on my mind is getting caught in a riptide. Oh, and then being taken by Jaws.

"Cool." He lightly grips the board on either side of his chest. "Now, as the wave's starting to roll, put your palms flat on the board. Push up. Then jump into a crouching position, feet about shoulder-width apart. You'll figure out which foot feels more natural to lead with. Rise up a little more. But keep your knees bent. You want a low center of gravity. Stick your arms out for balance. Head up. Eyes forward. And you're surfing. Well, standing up on your board anyway. Fancy stuff comes later."

"It's all really quick." I bite my lip.

"Try it. Double-time." He grins.

I perform the whole sequence so well the first time that he makes me do it six more times "to make sure it's not a fluke."

Unfortunately, once we're out on the water, the land-lubber in me sabotages my performance. The swell isn't even half a foot high, but I can't keep my balance. I spend more time treading water than I do paddling on the board.

"I'm not meant to be a creature of the sea," I pant. Alex looks at me with the patience of a saint. "Who knows? I could pioneer sand surfing instead."

"Yeah, I can totally see that as an Olympic sport some day." His smile brings dimples to his cheeks. It's really quite adorable the way that happens. Forget bulging pec muscles. Dimples really get my heart pumping.

Um, Molly? Focus on not drowning, okay?

"Should we call time for today?" I ask.

"Sure, but I'm telling you now," he says. "I've finally found my life's purpose. Teaching you to surf like a pro."

My heart pumps again, but this time painfully and sorrowfully. Six months is not a lot of time. It'll take me six months alone to learn how to stand up on a surfboard. Looking away, I nod, unable to utter coherent words.

Exhausted, I wade to the shallows and collapse on the sand with the board. I don't care about the sand coating my hair and neck. I'm just grateful to be alive. Alex flops beside me, breathing hard. We lie there for what feels like forever Nothing to bother us except the sounds of waves constantly approaching and retreating, squawking seagulls, and traffic building on the PCH behind us. I doze off long enough to dream of Alex, of him staring into my eyes with an intensity that makes my heart swell.

The sensation of something warm gliding along the back of my hand wakes me. I open one eye and find Alex gently rubbing my skin. He's staring at my fingers like he's trying to commit every line, every freckle to his memory.

I'm not sure if it's all the salt water I took in, but my throat's suddenly dry. I want to get some water, but even more, I want Alex to kiss me.

I want my best friend kiss to me right here, right now.

Talk about out of the blue.

"Hey," I whisper. Before I can talk myself out of it, I hook one hand around his neck and kiss him. Lightly. Enough to gauge his reaction. His warm, salty lips linger on mine, pressing gently at first, then with more delicious pressure. I can't get close enough to him. "Alex, this is..."

"Wait." Alex sits up. His cheeks are virtually on fire.

"What's wrong?" I thought he was enjoying the kiss. I sure as hell was.

"We should get going," he says without looking at me. "I've still got a bunch of things to do before I die."

He leaves me staring after him in shock.

I kissed my best friend.

And he walked away.

"DID you see the looks on those little kids' faces?! So worth it!" Alex says gleefully. We half-skip, half-walk down the corridor toward a waiting area and elevators. Visitors and hospital workers take one look at our woolly brown costumes and can't help but laugh out loud.

"They were totally confused." I twirl my long, curled tail. "I'm not so sure the kids bought our story about being Christmas kangaroos who got lost on the way to the North Pole. But they loved it. And they loved you."

"I don't know about that. Might've had something do with the toys we took out of our pouches." He waves goodbye to the oncology nurses one final time. They'd all been great about us coming in to read stories and hang out with patients. Of course, somehow Alex found the time to organize our visit to the unit in advance. We showed up looking like mutants from down under, and the staff didn't bat an eyelid.

I cast Alex a sidelong glance. Yesterday's kiss on the beach was yesterday's news. He hasn't mentioned it since. And I'm too cowardly to bring it up. I can only guess that he doesn't want to move our relationship to the next level because he doesn't see a future for us.

Why does life have to be this hard? Without warning, I start crying silently. I turn my head so Alex can't see.

"Alex? Wait." A nurse chases us down the hall.

"Did I forget something?" Alex squints and pats his marsupial pouch. While he's doing that, I discreetly wipe my eyes.

The nurse shakes her head. "One of the doctors peeked in when you were reading to the kids. Dr. Khan? She said she knows you from way back."

Alex breaks into huge grin. "Dr. Khan still works here?"

"She did a long stint in Britain, but she's been back for a couple of weeks," the nurse explains. "If you're okay with waiting for a few minutes while she finishes a consult, she'd love to come by and say hi."

Alex raises his eyebrows. "Is that cool with you, Molly?"

"Absolutely!" I say after clearing the husk out my voice.

We sit side by side on armchairs. Big plate-glass windows look out onto Ventura Boulevard and a row of pawnshops. Not the greatest of views from a children's hospital. But inside, the walls are painted a sunny yellow and enhanced with framed finger paintings.

Alex's knee jiggles uncontrollably. Beside him, I wage an internal struggle. I could tell him to stop it or I could put my hand on his leg. Or both. Until the past few days, I'd never thought too much about touching Alex. Now I feel like I can't keep my hands off him. When he was reading to the kids, I found myself sneaking looks at him and not being able to tear my gaze away. The kids were completely bewitched by him and the funny faces he pulled as he read.

I clamp a palm on his hyperactive leg. "Hey, are you nervous about meeting up with your old doctor?"

"Yeah." He gives a weak smile and puts his hand over mine. "Dr. Khan was *the* best. She's the one who inspired me to grow up and become a pediatrician. I even told her that I wanted to go to Yale, her alma mater. Now I know it's never gonna happen."

"But this could be great, Alex. She could have that sixth opinion we were looking for!"

A small woman with sleek black hair and a white coat gets out of an elevator. She glances around the waiting room and makes a beeline for Alex.

"Dr. Khan!" Alex practically hops toward her.

"Alex Gibson! It really is you!" The doctor widens her smile. She hugs him, but her short arms can only get halfway around his costume.

"I can't believe you remembered me after all this time!" he says in a voice that carries the slightest of tremors.

"You have changed some since I was last here as a resident, but I never forget a face." Dr. Khan laughs. "The tail is new."

"Stranger things have happened during puberty." Alex beckons me. I struggle out of the chair and pad over on my giant paws. "This is my best friend, Molly."

"Hi, Molly. It was nice of you two to come down and cheer up the kids. The nurses told me all about it." The doctor shakes my hand and smiles warmly. "So tell me, what else have you been doing? You must be close to graduating from high school."

Alex looks down at the purple carpet. I can almost tell what's running through his mind. For some reason, he's balking at confessing to a cancer doctor that he has cancer. In a super-bright and chipper voice, he says, "Yep, in my junior year. I've been working hard in my AP classes so I can get into Yale. Follow in your footsteps, you know?"

Dr. Khan looks from Alex to me, then back to Alex. "Oh, my goodness. Really? Alex, I know you'll get there. You have such drive and determination. Listen, let me have your email address. I'd be happy to write a character reference for you."

The doctor types Alex's address into her phone as he recites it. A disembodied voice calls her name over the P.A.

"I'm so sorry, Alex. Duty calls." She gives both of us quick hug. "It was so wonderful to see you again. I'm really proud of you. I'll send that reference this afternoon, okay?"

We watch her hurry to the nurses' station, then disappear around a corner.

"Alex, why didn't you tell her?" I feel itchy and sweaty not just from the costume, but from anxiety.

He gulps and shrugs. "I wanted that character reference. If only to get into heaven or whatever comes next."

Tears prickle my eyes. Again. "But she could help you stay on earth a little longer."

"Molly, I'm not going to get better. I can feel it in my bones." Slowly, he turns to me. "I've figured out what my next bucket list item is."

"You have?" I dam a tear with my finger. He looks at the floor, seemingly in no hurry to elaborate. "Don't leave me in suspense. What is it?"

He lowers his voice. "Plan a sustainable funeral."

I splutter. "Alex, no."

"I've gotta put together a playlist. Maybe pick out a coffin. A shroud or sustainable cardboard. What do you think?"

"Stop it. You can't joke about this stuff."

His eyes flashed. "I'm not. I'm being practical. The last thing I want is for my mom and dad to think about planning the minutiae of my send-off. It has to be as easy as possible for them."

"It's not going to be easy, whether organize very last detail or not," I say in a subdued voice. On one hand, it's admirable that he wants to minimize the pain for his parents. And on the other hand, I can't handle the idea that in the very near future.

"No." Alex looks down at me sadly, his little kangaroo ears flopping as he moves. He shuffles away to greet another patient, leaving me staring after him, my heart in my throat.

Alex may think he's reached a dead end. He's been in and out of treatment for so long. He's beyond exhausted. But I've got enough physical and mental willpower for us both. There *has* to be a way forward—one that doesn't include a funeral any time soon.

TWELVE

Alex

"How did you pull this together so fast?" Molly gapes, clearly impressed by my work. Her pixie face, framed by that short crop of shiny dark hair, radiates joy.

"Not bad for T-minus 62, huh?" I smile. Head tilted to the ornate ceiling, she spins around and around. Chrome and frosted glass light fittings on the walls give the room a soft yellow aura.

Tom really came through for me. Or rather, his movie mogul parents did. They pulled a helluva lot of strings so I could use their big-time studio's screening room. It was less risky than having me get behind the wheel of Tom's 911.

"Some day, we're going to be saying T-*plus* 62, et cetera, et cetera," she says, waving a hand dismissively. I love her show of optimism, I really do.

Things have settled in the past couple of days. She freaked out about the bone cancer diagnosis. Freaked. I know she's trying hard to keep those feelings under wraps now. Me? I'm back at the acceptance stage and am done with freaking out.

"Speaking of positive figures, whew, you look incredible." I told her to go vintage-dress shopping and find something that screamed HOLLYWOOD! She dug up a slinky, silky gold number Natalie Wood would've worn back in the day.

"Oooh, you're so smooth! Thanks." Almost shyly, she adds, "You look red-carpet ready yourself in that suit."

"A present from Dad." It's a special night, so I don't tell her I plan to be buried in this suit. But I'll go to my grave knowing she approves of it.

Her eyes glisten. "Must be great to have him back in L.A."

"Yeah, at last. He says he can easily run his business from here. Even Mom's happy to see him again. I think they'll need each other. You know, after I'm gone." I quickly clear a lump from my throat and put on my best TV personality voice. "Did you know this is where the bigwigs and actors used to watch the rushes? The stuff they shot that day? So watch where you sit. Might find James Dean's fifty-year-old chewing gum under an armrest."

She laughs like it's the most hilarious thing ever, and that makes me light up inside. "If I do, I'll auction it off for charity."

When she kissed me on the beach, at first I was stunned. After all these years, I finally got to kiss Molly. But at the same time, that kiss tore me up. Did she do it because she felt sorry for me? In the end, I had to get away, because it seemed pointless to start something that's got zero chance of surviving.

That was a mistake. I've been punishing myself ever since that day.

"So it's just us tonight?" She sweeps her arm across the ten-seat theater. Red velvet curtains with gold tassels hide the movie screen. The whole place is no bigger than my living room. Cozy and intimate. Perfect for tonight.

Pointing to the back of the room, I say, "You, me and the projectionist. He promised to leave us alone for the most part."

She claps her hands together. "What are we watching?"

"An oldie but a goodie. I think you might know it." I catch sight of the projectionist through the portholes as he laces film over and under rollers.

Molly's eyes go round. "Rebel Without a Cause!"

"I know. Again. But maybe this time don't talk all the way through or chomp on popcorn, okay? It's not like we can press rewind here."

Molly swats me playfully.

"And it's an old print, too. Scratches and everything. Makes it even more of an old-Hollywood experience." I lead Molly to a seat in the center of the room, in line with speakers on the walls. A silver bowl filled with salty-sweet popcorn rests on the empty chair beside her.

"Alex, this is perfect. You've thought of everything."

"I've learned from the queen of organizing," I say. "All settled?"

"Yeah, let's get this show on the road. Double-time." She giggles.

"Watch this." I press a button on my armrest. "Mr. Grant? My starlet here would like the movie to roll now."

"Sure thing, boss," comes the projectionist's gruff voice over an intercom.

The lights dim and the velvet curtain parts. Dramatic orchestral music crashes into our eardrums. I glance at Molly. Her skin glows red, the color of the letters shouting the movie title on the screen. She gets deeply engrossed within minutes like she'd never seen it before. After a while, her head drops onto my shoulder and stays there. Every breath, every sigh, every gasp she makes seems louder than the dialogue.

I stare at the screen, but the images are a blur. I'm not interested in the teenage angst up there. I'm thinking about *my* inner teen angst. Exactly when is the right time to tell someone you're in love with them? Is there a wrong time? When James Dean is crying in a scene? When the Grim Reaper is hot on your tail?

I've prepared myself for all possible reactions. Molly doesn't have to say she loves me back. She could even walk out on me if she wants to. But I need her to know how I feel before I die.

Molly shifts suddenly. Her right leg angles closer to mine. I hesitate for a few seconds, then close the gap with my thigh so we're touching. Feeling bold—'cause what have I got to lose, right?—I inch my hand over and hold hers. She doesn't move away. That's good.

In my head, I rehearse the words I want to tell her after the movie: "I love you."

Then something weird happens.

Molly stops breathing.

That's not good.

I sit up quickly, my grip tightening around her hand. "Molly?"

In a stunned whisper, she asks, "What did you say?"

Dumbfounded, I stare at her. "I... I said your name. I wanted to check you were still alive 'cause you stopped breathing for a second."

"No, before that." Her green eyes lock on me, and I can't look away.

"I didn't say anything. Or at least I don't think so." I frown. Did I actually say the words aloud instead of in my head? Am I that big a doofus?

"Are you sure? I could have sworn you said, 'I love you.'"

Looking down, I realize I'm still holding her hand. Her pulse matches mine. Fast and pounding.

This is it. *This* is the right time. While there's crazy shouting going on in the movie. While I'm buzzing with nervous energy. While I've got Molly right here beside me, where she's been practically my entire life.

I take in as much air as my lungs will hold. She watches me intently. "You didn't imagine it. I said I love you, Molly Corbett. I always have loved you. I'll love you till the very end."

Holding my breath, I wait for her to throw the bowl of popcorn over my head. Run out on me. Or worse, laugh.

"Ohhh, Alex!" Two tears roll down each cheek. One drop for her, one for me. "I love you, too."

"You do? Are you sure?"

"Don't ask me dumb questions at a time like this," she murmurs. "Kiss me."

Leaning forward, I kiss her tears away, then trail my lips down to Molly's. Her arms wrap around me, and I squeeze as hard as I can without strangling a vital organ. All I want is to keep her as close as possible for as long as possible.

Then a jarring thought distracts me. I pull back and she squints. "This could be another dumb question. Did you say you love me just because I'm dying?"

"Yes, that's a really dumb question," she says solemnly. Linking her fingers around my neck, she drags me close again. Her kiss is light as a feather, but the impact is huge. "I love you because you make me happy even when you're infuriating. You make me happy by walking into my room with a bag of popcorn. Wait, you don't even have to bring popcorn! Just yourself. You're lovable, adorable and, I'm very, very happy to report, a thousand times kissable."

Orchestral music swells around my ears. Our lips dance together. Moving fast, moving slow. Yes, *this* was the perfect moment to tell her how I felt.

The next time we look up at the screen, the words *The End* appear. Gradually, the lights go up. Hands entwined, Molly and I stare at the curtains as they glide shut once more.

A strange peace settles over me, and not just because the chaos in the movie is finally silenced.

Mr. Grant's voice crackles over the intercom. "Hope you enjoyed that, folks. I'm gonna wrap a few things up here and I'll meet you out in the foyer in fifteen minutes."

Molly leans over and presses the button. "Thank you!" She winks at me. "Do you think he saw us making out for the entire movie?"

"Nah. He was probably checking Facebook the whole time." I clear throat. "So, Molly… telling you I love you, that was number five."

"From your bucket list?" Her eyes widen. "It's not going to be the last time you tell me, is it?"

"No. I'll tell you every hour, on the hour, from now on."

Molly angles her head in confusion. "Let's go over this list. One, getting gravel rash on a bike trail. Two, teaching me to surf. Three, the hospital visit. Four, confessing you're madly in love with me, and I'm glad you did because I'm mad about you. Five…?"

Sheepishly, I tell her, "Go back one step. Four. I sent my application to Yale."

Molly squeals. "You did?! I'm so proud of you!"

I silence her with a kiss. This is how I wanted to kiss her on the beach. Slow, fast, hard, soft. For a very long time. But I was saving myself for tonight.

What the hell was I thinking? Short answer: I wasn't thinking.

"Can I make another confession?" I take her soft moan as a yes. "Technically, 'Kiss Molly Corbett' has been number one on my bucket list since we were thirteen."

She grins. "It was worth the wait. For me anyway."

"And me." I stroke her cheek.

"We'll make up for it." Molly leans her forehead against mine. "You know what we're gonna do? Make another list of five things we haven't done before. And then another list when we get through those."

Hugging her tight, I say, "But no more of this double-time, double-speed stuff. Too dangerous. From now on, we take things super slowly."

"That might take some practice."

"I'm willing to put in the work."

Molly chuckles. She tilts her head, bringing her lips toward mine but not quite touching. Her breath breezes across my face. We're so close, yet so far apart. I can't stand it anymore, that millimeter-wide gap between us. I kiss her slowly, deliberately, starting with faint pressure that builds and builds. My pulse starts to race, and as I cup her slender neck, I can feel hers galloping, too.

Later, when we pull apart, I'm so dazed I can't even remember what planet we're on. I whisper, "Yep, that's more my speed."

THIRTEEN

Molly

Alex is gonna flip. I grin to myself while closing the email from Dr. Khan. And when Alex is well enough, he'll also spring into a succession of somersaults, triple pikes, and probably even bungee jumps.

I'm parked outside Forever Sustainable, the discreet, eco-friendly funeral home on La Brea, waiting for Alex to show. Not exactly thrilled about *this* bucket list location. But it's his life, not mine. I have my own long list of wishes, and thanks to Dr. Khan, one of them could come true.

I reopen the mail app on my phone.

"You mentioned Alex's dad lives in Australia," the doctor's message read. *"There's an exciting gene-therapy trial underway there. I'm reluctant to use the word 'cure.' However, early results are looking quite promising for people with Alex's type of cancer. I'd be happy to chat with Alex and his parents. Let me know."*

Drumming my fingers on the steering wheel, I mull over my options. If I were in Mrs. G.'s shoes, in *Alex's* shoes, I'd want to know if a potentially life-saving treatment was available. Maybe she already knows about it. Maybe not. Either way, it'd be irresponsible of me to not tell her what I learned from the doc, right? Right. I fire off a message to Mrs. G.

Minutes later, Alex pulls up. He's barely out of the Toyota before I jump on him.

"What are you so happy about?" Alex laughs, leaning back against the doorframe.

I wind my arms around his neck. "Seriously? You really need to ask after what happened at our very private movie screening last night?"

He angles his face down and kisses me, making my heart float like a butterfly. When he pulls back, he says in a husky voice, "So this thing between us is really happening? It's not my imagination?"

"You do have a vivid imagination, but this *thing* is totally happening." I punctuate the sentence with a kiss.

Another car enters the lot. Its screeching brakes jolt us back to reality. Alex closes his car door and stares at the funeral home's signage. A simple green logo features a stylized tree. Roots curl downward to embrace a horizontal rectangle. No mistaking it's meant to depict a coffin buried six feet under.

"Ready?" Alex asks, gaze glued to the storefront.

I gulp. "No."

He doesn't move a muscle. "Me neither."

"We don't have to do this now," I whisper. Strange how our roles have reversed. Usually, I'm the plotter and planner, whereas Alex goes with the flow.

"There's no point in putting it off. The last thing I want is for Mom to get lumped with picking out an eco-friendly coffin after I kick it."

I breathe in sharply. "You can decide on a... a coffin another day."

"We're running out of time," comes his strained reply.

Squeezing his arm hard enough to make him grimace, I say, "There's one more treatment option we could try. Dr. Khan told me there's a clinical trial that's going on in Australia. Something to do with gene editing. It targets certain kinds of cancers and they're seeing positive results so far."

Annoyance flickers across his face. He takes a step away. "Hold up, hold up. You spoke with Dr. Khan?"

"Yeah." I fold my arms. "I figured there was no harm in asking if she'd heard about any treatments could help you."

"It's none of your business."

"Of course it is! I care about you. I *love* you. I'm not giving up on you without a fight. And you shouldn't either."

A matte-gray SUV with dark tinted windows pulls up a few car spaces away. Moments later, the occupants emerge —a brunette woman wearing enormous sunglasses and two middle-grade aged boys. A family of three. Judging by their lost, shattered expressions, perhaps they were a family of four until very recently.

"Mom, I don't want to go in," cries the youngest of the boys. He holds onto his mother's hand, dragging her back.

"Robbie, it's okay," says the other boy. "We'll do this together. We'll make Dad proud."

My heart cracks as the mother's shoulders sag visibly.

She catches herself, neatens her messy bun, and speaks in a clear voice. "Nate's right, Robbie. Come on, we can all be strong for Daddy."

Alex and I watch them lean together and move as one into the funeral home. When the doors fully shut behind the family, I sneak a look at Alex. Is he thinking what I'm thinking? That we've got to grab every opportunity that comes our way, because we'll never truly know how much time we have left?

"Australia, huh?" Alex says faintly.

I swallow. "Yeah. At a clinic in Sydney, not far from where your dad lives."

He stares into space for the longest time. I can almost hear the cogs in his brain grinding and groaning. "I can't afford to go."

"You can," I say, putting steel into my voice. "I'll host a bake sale to raise money. Maybe even put together a cook-book. Plus, I'm a hundred percent sure your parents will do anything to get you there."

"You spoke to them, too?" he says, but this time with less annoyance.

"Kinda. I messaged your mom today."

Alex shudders and winces.

My chest tightens with alarm. "Are you in pain?"

"No. I was just saying a prayer." A teasing smile lifts a corner of his mouth. "Remember those lemon bars you made for Christmas last year? Legit could've built a quake-proof wall out of them."

Filled with faux outrage, I push him. Lightly. His criti-cism of my past baking efforts was fair. Even I had to admit I could've cracked a tooth on those lemon bars. "Ye of little faith! I've tested and retested a dozen new recipes. Believe me, we'll make a fortune out of my cookies."

"I believe you." He leans forward and kisses me deeply. When we draw apart, hope and gratitude sparkle in his eyes. "I'm starting to believe in a lot of things."

EPILOGUE

Alex

I'll admit it. I was pissed at Molly for pushing yet another treatment on me. I'd made peace with dying. Even welcomed it when the meds couldn't take the pain away. Now, at T-*plus* 420 days, I'm standing on top of the Sydney Harbour Bridge. I'm closer to heaven now than I was a year ago, yet further from death. Thanks to the researchers. Thanks to the doctors, the nurses, my parents. Thanks most of all to Molly, who I'm never pissed at for more than a minute.

As of today, I'm officially in remission. There's always going to be a physical ache where the cancer once gnawed away at my body. In a weird way, I almost relish that ache. It reminds me I'm still alive, still around to do what I love, and be with the people I love.

A breeze whips through my hair. Easing my grip on the thick rails, I sway. It had taken two hours to follow our group leader to the bridge's summit. I take in the gleaming white sails of the Opera House far below. Vintage green-

and-yellow ferries charge with determination over the glittering, choppy water. They're overshadowed by a multistory cruise ship, ten times the size of the *Titanic*.

Dressed in a gray jumpsuit identical to mine and tethered to safety cables, Molly gazes down at Circular Quay. Almost 50 meters above sea level, she's showing no fear of heights. Not even a tremble. Her face is glowing with joy. Or maybe it's just the sheen of the zinc sunblock she'd slathered on in our hotel room.

"Let's go on a cruise next spring break," Molly yells. She'd worked so freaking hard to get us both into Yale. Yet for some reason, she spends an awful lot of time organizing trips away from the place.

"Sounds good!" Though I hate the idea of being stuck on the high seas for weeks on end, I add *Caribbean cruise* to my never-ending bucket list. Nothing's off limits these days. "You realize you'll have to run at least a hundred more bake sales to pay for that, right?"

"I'll start planning as soon as we get off this giant coathanger," she says, referring to locals' nickname for the arched steel bridge. "You can help me this time. And not just as chief taste-tester, okay?"

"Do I get danger money for that job?"

Molly sidles closer to me. "No, but you get me."

"Forever?" I murmur.

Molly smiles. "And ever."

BONUS CONTENT

MRS. G'S KALE RECIPES

Dear Moll-Moll,

I was so pleased to see how much you enjoyed my kale and broccoli smoothie. Don't you feel healthy and energized now? I thought I'd send a few special recipes for you to try. You're welcome.

FAITH & LOVE & KALE SMOOTHIE

Ingredients:

1/2 cup broccoli florets, raw

1 cup kale, raw

1/2 medium-sized cucumber, sliced and diced

1/2 cup chilled coconut water or coconut milk if you're feeling adventurous

1/4 cup goji berries

Method:

Whizz the broccoli, kale, cucumber, and goji berries in a blender. Gradually add the coconut water or milk until, well, smooth and drinkable. Pour into a tall glass. Alex tends to down this while melodramatically pinching his nose, but I know he secretly adores this smoothie.

Slippery Sautéed Kale & Mushrooms
Ingredients:
1 tbsp butter
2 tbsp olive oil
1 clove garlic, crushed
1 cup button mushrooms, sliced thinly
2 cups kale
A small splash of balsamic vinegar
Salt & pepper to taste

Method:
Heat the olive oil in a frying pan or wok. Add the butter and allow it to melt. Then toss the garlic to this shimmery golden pool. As the garlic begins to brown, throw in the mushrooms. Stir until soft. Splash in the balsamic vinegar and kale. Keep stirring. Lob in more butter if necessary. When the kale is wilted and "slimy," as Alex would say, season with salt and pepper, and serve. This is divine on sourdough toast or with scrambled eggs.

Kale Ice-Cream Dream*

Ingredients:
2/3 cup condensed milk
1 1/4 cup heavy cream
1 cup kale, cooked and pureed (ensure you squeeze as much liquid out as possible)

Method:
In a large bowl, whip the condensed milk and cream

together until well combined. Fold in the puréed kale. Pour the blended green mixture into a 2-pint container or two 1-pint containers. Freeze overnight. Enjoy for breakfast.

*All right, I admit I'm only kidding about this one. But I think it'd make Alex smile, so I beg you to give it a try.

Mrs. G. xoxo

ABOUT THE AUTHOR

Australian Vanessa Barneveld lives in a 19th-century house in inner-city Sydney with a 21st-century husband, two eccentric cats and one ghost—all of whom provide inspiration for her spirited novels. Her debut Young Adult novel, This Is Your Afterlife, won Oklahoma Romance Writers of America's National Readers' Choice Award.

In addition to her writing career, she's part of a crack team that produces closed captions for deaf TV viewers and audio descriptions for the blind. An avid traveler, she enjoys the journeys almost as much as the destinations.

vanessabarneveld.com